Also by the Author

The Erin O'Reilly Mysteries
Black Velvet
Irish Car Bomb
White Russian
Double Scotch (coming soon)

The Clarion Chronicles
Ember of Dreams

White Russian

The Erin O'Reilly Mysteries
Book Three

Steven Henry

Clickworks Press • Baltimore, MD

First publication: Clickworks Press, 2018
Release: CWP-EOR3-INT-P.IS-1.2

Sign up for updates, deals, and exclusive sneak peeks at clickworkspress.com/join.

ISBN-10: 1-943383-43-X
ISBN-13: 978-1-943383-43-6

For my mom and dad, Carl and Mary Caroline Henry, and for the books they read to me when I was young.

White Russian

Pour 5 parts vodka and 2 parts Kahlua into an old fashioned glass filled with ice. Shake 3 parts fresh cream to thicken it. Pour cream on top of drink. Stir slowly and serve.

Chapter 1

Erin O'Reilly was facing one of the toughest challenges of her career. She was a detective in the NYPD. She'd been in gunfights, helped disarm explosives, fought desperate criminals, and had her hands stained with the blood of a dying man. But that was nothing compared with finding an affordable apartment in Manhattan.

The commute from Queens was killing her. The subway wouldn't have been too bad, but she had a take-home squad car. She could leave the car at the precinct, but then she'd have no good way to transport Rolf. He was a great partner, the best she'd had, but he had special needs, most of them having to do with his being a ninety-pound German Shepherd. She'd taken him on the subway a couple times, but it wasn't something to make a habit of.

Erin liked Queens. It was where she'd been born and where she'd spent most of her eleven years as a cop. She loved the blue-collar, salt-of-the-earth feel of the place. She knew the streets like an old friend, and could pick up on anything out of the ordinary the moment she saw it.

But she was a downtown cop now, working an experimental Major Crimes unit. She'd stuck out her neck to catch an art thief, and it had brought her to the attention of the big boys. It was more glamorous, maybe, but she sometimes missed walking a beat. Even showing up to work in slacks and a civilian blouse still didn't feel normal. In any case, she had to find a place to live on the other side of the East River.

Initial scouting wasn't promising. In the whole United States, only San Francisco had a more insane real-estate market. After looking up some pretty small apartments, and comparing their rent with her monthly salary, she just about gave up. And then there was the need to have Rolf there, plus parking for her Charger. It was hopeless.

Then she'd figured out what she was doing wrong. She was trying to crack the case on the weight of hard evidence alone, when there wasn't enough of it to go on. She needed an informant, and that meant talking to the locals. She started with the other cops at Precinct 8.

It was Bob Michaelson, a veteran Patrol sergeant, who gave her the best shot at a break. "Yeah, I know a guy," he said. "Runs a place near Columbus Park. Just a few blocks from here. Has a view of the park and everything. Couple nice bars real close. Lemme give him a call, see what I can find out."

Erin didn't think too much of it at the time, but Michaelson dropped by the following day, just as she was starting to pack up for the night. "Hey, O'Reilly, here you go," he said, dropping a folded piece of paper onto her desk. There was a Bayard Street address penciled on it. "I know the landlord. Tell him Bob says hi."

Now, at the end of a long workday, she stood outside an apartment in south Manhattan, Rolf's leash in one hand, wondering if it was even worth asking. She shrugged and buzzed the super's intercom.

"Yeah? Whaddaya want?" a surly voice demanded.

"I'm looking for an apartment," she said. Then, feeling a little silly, she added, "Bob told me to talk to you."

"Okay, sure," the super said. His tone changed at once. "C'mon in." The door clicked open.

The superintendent was a jowly, beefy guy. "Preston Harris," he said, offering his hand.

"Erin O'Reilly," she said, shaking. Then she added, out of force of habit, "NYPD."

Her police instincts caught the sidelong look he shot her as he led her inside. But he didn't say anything. Maybe he'd heard of her from the news. She'd made the papers with the art heist in Queens, and again not long ago when she'd solved a bomb plot while managing not to blow up a sizable chunk of Manhattan.

"Here ya go," he said, opening the door to the apartment. "Third floor, one-bedroom, full bath. Have a look round."

Erin knew right away it had been a mistake to come here. She wanted it too much. There was easily twice the square footage of her studio apartment in Queens. The carpet was fairly new and didn't have any significant stains. The kitchen was clean with recently-installed fridge and microwave. Even the bathroom was spotless and well-kept.

"I've got my K-9," she said, twitching Rolf's leash. "Is that gonna be a problem?"

"Nah, no problem," Harris said. "Hey, it's good having a cop in the building. Keeps petty crime down. And two cops, even better, right? Drives up the property values."

"How much you asking?" Erin asked, bracing herself.

"Twelve-fifty."

She hadn't heard him right. That was the only possibility. "No way," she said.

"Hey," Harris said, putting his palms out. "I gotta make a living here. I can maybe go down to twelve even, but that's it."

Something was fishy. Twelve hundred dollars? The average

cost of a southeastern Manhattan apartment was more than twice that. Erin put her hands on her hips and stared at Harris, trying to figure him out. "You got a lot of gang activity around here?" she asked. That would explain both the low asking price and his desire to have a cop in residence.

"Well, not so's you'd notice," Harris said. "You'll be fine here. Look, is there a problem? Something you don't like?"

"No, no, it's fine," Erin said.

"Then why don't I draw up the papers, just so they're ready," Harris said. "Hey, I don't wanna put pressure on you. But I think this is the place you wanna be."

She shrugged. "Sure." But she promised herself she'd take an extra-careful look around the place, just to make sure there weren't any broken pipes, meth labs, or angry ghosts before she signed a lease agreement. It still didn't add up, but Erin was coming off a long day at work and she was ready for something to go her way.

* * *

Now it was a week later, Thursday evening, and she was moving in, just like that. She didn't have too much stuff, but it was more than a one-person job. Fortunately, like Michaelson, she knew a guy. The guy was Vic Neshenko, the biggest, strongest man in Precinct 8 and a fellow detective on her squad. The Russian was glad to help carry her stuff up from Queens. As he put it, "Friends help you move. Partners help you move *bodies.*"

"I don't need any bodies moved," she said. "But I could use a hand with the box spring."

Vic borrowed a pickup from a guy he knew. Between that guy, Sergeant Michaelson, Preston Harris, and Vic himself, Erin was starting to understand something she'd been told by a mob guy not long before. The world really did run on favors.

They got started later than they wanted to. Getting down to Queens in rush hour just reminded her how glad she was that this was the last time she'd be doing it for a while. By the time they got back with the furniture loaded up, it was almost nine thirty and getting dark. They started with the boxes of books and clothes, leaving the heavy pieces for last. Erin's new apartment had a lot to recommend it, but the elevator was really small. That meant moving her bed up two flights of stairs. They were a little over halfway, and had just passed the second-floor landing, when Vic's phone started ringing.

"Shit," Vic said, shifting his grip.

"Just set it down," Erin muttered. "I got it."

Vic leaned the box spring against the wall. Erin held it there while he grabbed his phone out of his hip pocket. "Neshenko," he said. "No, sir, I'm still in town. Helping O'Reilly move. Yeah, she's here with me. Yes, sir. We'll be right there."

"What's up?" Erin asked. "Was that the Lieutenant?"

"Let's quick get this the rest of the way up," he said, grabbing his end of the bed again. "Then we've gotta get out to a Super 8 in Brooklyn. Guess we're not done working tonight."

"How bad?"

"Webb says it's a double homicide, multiple GSW," Vic said. "Automatic weapons. Sounds like a gang hit."

"Back to work," Erin said through gritted teeth, wrestling the springs up the last two steps to the third floor. "I was gonna buy you a drink," she added, "but I guess we'd better take a rain check."

"I could use one," Vic said. "But I've got a feeling I'll want it more later. I just hope there's no kids. I hate when kids get tagged."

Chapter 2

Vic and Erin rode to the motel together in Erin's Charger, Rolf in his back-seat compartment. They crossed the East River into Brooklyn on the famous bridge. Erin shook her head and stifled a laugh.

"What's funny?" Vic asked.

"I just finished moving into Manhattan," she said. "Now, my first night in my new place, and I'm spending it in Brooklyn. Not my idea of a celebration."

"Maybe we'll still have time for that drink," Vic said. "After."

It was full dark by the time they got to the motel. They knew the place before they even got close, from all the red and blue lights. It looked like seven or eight units had already responded. There was an ambulance, too, but as they pulled up they could see the paramedics leaning on the back fender looking bored. That wasn't a good sign.

Webb's Crown Victoria was in the lot, too. Erin saw the Lieutenant talking to a couple of uniforms outside the lobby. She hopped out of the Charger, fetched Rolf, and headed over to her CO.

"What's the situation, sir?" she asked.

"I see you brought Neshenko," Webb said. "Good." He looked even wearier and more cynical than usual. He had an unlit cigarette in one hand, forgotten. "I just talked to the ME. She's on her way, should be here in ten to fifteen."

He sighed. "It's bad. We've got two victims, DOA. The medics didn't even bother trying to patch them up. The night manager heard gunfire. She thought it was a movie at first, until she heard the screaming and bullets came through the wall into the hallway." He jerked a thumb in the direction of the lobby. A young woman was sitting in a chair next to a uniformed officer. The woman was crying. "It's a ground-floor room, number 103," he went on. "Jones is there now, securing the scene."

"Okay, let's check it out," Erin said.

Webb nodded. "Carefully, people." They crossed the lobby into the hallway.

"Good thing nobody was walking here," Vic observed. The wall to their right was riddled with holes. Chunks of plaster and ribbons of cheap wallpaper were scattered all over the floor.

"Hey, guys. Took your time getting here." Kira Jones waved from the doorway of room 103. She was dressed for a night on the town, from her high-heeled boots and miniskirt to her spiked hair, which was dyed dark red with blue tips. Erin had heard the precinct had a pool running on how many tattoos she had hidden under her clothes.

"Jesus, I can smell the gunpowder from here," Vic said.

"No shit," Jones said. "Have a look."

They gathered in the doorway, looking into what had been a cheap motel room. Now it was a war zone. Bullet holes were everywhere, perforating the queen-size bed and wood-veneer furniture. An uneven line of jagged holes angled across the TV screen. Cartridge casings were scattered across the carpet, most of them near the window. The window itself was shattered into tiny shards.

And there were the bodies. Two of them, a man and a woman. They lay close together, beside the bed. The man was face-down, wearing a shirt that'd been white when he'd put it on but was now dark red. He had on very nice shoes and black slacks. The woman was on her back, clad in a bright red dress that did a better job of hiding the bloodstains. One black stiletto heel was still on her foot. She'd kicked off the other shoe, maybe as a dying reflex. That shoe, lying in a dark bloodstain on the carpet, caught Erin's eye. For some reason, it was the worst detail in the room, that bare foot with the toes thrusting toward the ceiling. It was even worse than the woman's wide-open eyes, or the bullet hole in the middle of her forehead.

"Wow," Erin said.

"That's a hell of a lot of bullets," Vic said, indicating the room with a sweep of his hand.

Webb was crouching down, looking at a cartridge casing. ".45 caliber," he said.

"MAC-10?" Jones suggested.

"More than one," Erin said. There were just too many bullet holes. A MAC-10 submachine-gun could spit out plenty of lead, but it only held thirty bullets in a magazine. There were way more than thirty holes.

"I'm thinking three shooters," Vic said. "Maybe more. Window?"

"Yeah," Erin agreed. The damage to the room was all on the half away from the window. She carefully crossed the room, avoiding stepping on any of the debris or bodies. Rolf daintily picked up his paws, sniffing at everything in his path. She leaned out the window. As she'd suspected, she saw a whole lot more cartridge casings. "Looks like they opened fire from here, through the glass," she reported.

"It wasn't a drive-by," Webb said. "They had to dismount, otherwise most of the brass would still be in the car. And with more brass inside, at least one of them climbed inside and kept shooting."

"So at least three guys come up, look in the window, and blast through it," Jones said. "Then what? They come into the room? Why?"

"They had to make sure," Erin said. She turned at the window and stared into the room, seeing how it would have looked from outside. "I can't even see the bodies from here. They fell behind the bed. Maybe they were dead, maybe not, but the shooters wouldn't have been able to tell from here."

"I got an empty mag out here," one of the uniforms said helpfully. "Looks like it came from an automatic weapon."

"Christ," Vic said. "They *reloaded*? I guess they had to. MAC-10s go through bullets like junkies through heroin."

"Okay," Erin said, walking through it. "At least one of them reloads outside. They climb in through the window, go around the foot of the bed, look down, and finish them off."

"No bullet holes in the floor," Webb pointed out. "Look at the male's position. He tried to get up and run. They gunned him down before he got to the door. I'm thinking he ducked the first volley, then got hit later."

"Right in the back," Vic said. "Bastards. Mob hit. It's gotta be. Shitty marksmanship, though, if they didn't hit him on the first try."

"Maybe he was quick," Erin said. "Or he might've gotten wounded but could still run."

Movement in the doorway caught their attention. All four detectives saw Sarah Levine, the Medical Examiner. Unlike the other investigators, she looked like she'd come straight from the precinct. She had her lab coat and gloves on, ready to do business.

"Glad we didn't wake you up," Webb said.

"Huh?" Levine asked blankly. "No, I was awake. I'm

working nights this week. Where's the dead guy?"

"Her boyfriend's a doctor," Jones explained to Erin in an undertone. "She tries to coordinate schedules with him."

"She's got a boyfriend?" Erin whispered, astonished. Levine wasn't unattractive, but she was one of the most poorly-socialized women she'd ever met.

"Hey, there's someone for everyone," Jones replied with a wink.

Levine took a good, long look at the bodies.

"Got a cause of death for us, Doc?" Vic asked with a sardonic smile.

"Not yet," Levine said.

"That was a joke, Doc," Vic said. "We know the cause of death."

Levine looked up. "Okay, Detective. What killed her?"

"A whole bunch of .45 slugs," Vic said.

"No."

Vic blinked. "You telling me she was already dead? Or she died of something else? Tell you what. Maybe she had a heart attack. Or how about cancer? Really, really fast-acting cancer?"

Levine wasn't good at sarcasm. "I won't know about underlying medical conditions until I do the bloodwork and the autopsy," she said. "But I can see she's got at least three bullet wounds to her legs and lower abdomen. Those didn't kill her. What killed her is this." She took a pencil out of her lab coat's pocket and pointed to the hole in the middle of the woman's forehead.

"That's what I said," Vic said.

"You said .45 slugs killed her," Levine said. "This hole's too small for a .45. I'd say nine-millimeter."

"Nine-millimeter," Erin echoed, scanning the floor of the room. There wasn't as much spent brass in here as outside, but it still took her a minute to find the one that was different. Then she saw it. The shell casing had flown a surprising distance, ending up at the base of the TV stand. "I've got it here," she said, stooping to take a closer look. "One nine-millimeter pistol casing. Looks a little funny, though. Not quite like a standard nine."

"There's powder tattooing around the entry wound," Levine said. "The gun was almost contact close. Probably less than a meter."

"Execution style," Webb said.

"What about the guy?" Vic asked.

"He's got five shots in the back," Levine said. "Both lungs perforated, along with a heart shot. He was dead by the time he hit the ground."

"So they mowed down the guy, then took out the girl to eliminate the witness," Vic said.

"Either that, or she was the target," Erin suggested.

"She's a hooker," Webb said. "Look at the clothes."

"What's that got to do with it?" Jones retorted. "People kill hookers all the time."

"Prostitutes get knifed or beaten to death," Webb said. "Not blown away with machine guns. Ten bucks says when we ID this guy, he's gonna be a mobster."

"No bet," Vic said.

"I'll take some of that action," Erin said. She was staring at the young face of the woman—more of a girl, really. "I got ten says you're wrong, sir."

Chapter 3

"Okay," Webb said. "Jones, you and I will talk to the manager. Neshenko, see about ID on the victims. O'Reilly, you and your K-9 get as much of a whiff of the perps as you can. Let's get to work, people."

Erin didn't have high hopes, but she took Rolf to the window. "*Such*," she said. Rolf had been born in Bavaria and had been trained in German. It had been easier for her to learn the foreign commands than to re-train the dog. Rolf, tail wagging, sniffed at the windowsill, then took off into the parking lot.

The whole thing was a waste of time, Erin knew. The shooters hadn't walked to the motel, and they sure hadn't walked away after emptying about a hundred bullets into the room. Rolf couldn't track a car. But she got a surprise. The dog paused at a storm drain and snuffled at the grating. He glanced up at her, tail waving expectantly.

"Hey!" Erin shouted to the nearest cops. A couple of patrolmen hurried over.

"What's up, Detective?" one asked.

She still wasn't used to being called that, and she couldn't help liking the sound of it. "We need to take a look down there," she said, pointing to the grating. "I think they might've chucked something down it."

"Fantastic," muttered one of the uniforms. "Let's go digging in the mud." But the guys got down to it without too much bitching. Meanwhile, Rolf headed on, following his nose.

After that, it was the anticlimax she'd expected. He lost the scent at a parking place in the darkest corner of the lot. He went back and forth, sniffing the blacktop, then stopped and whined unhappily.

"Good boy," she said, scratching him behind the ears and handing him his rubber Kong ball. He'd given it his best shot. She played her flashlight over the space as Rolf dropped to the pavement and happily chewed at his toy. The search wasn't a total washout. She saw the marks left by the tires of a car that had pulled out in a hurry. They almost certainly belonged to the getaway vehicle. Most people didn't burn rubber pulling out of a motel parking slot. She labeled the rubber spots with a couple of numbered yellow plastic markers. There were security cameras in the lot. Maybe they'd get some footage they could use to ID the vehicle, and the tread-marks might be useful to the CSU guys.

She canvassed the area around the parking spot, hoping for something that'd been carelessly left behind, and came up with a cigarette butt. Unlike every other cig Erin had seen, this one was black and gold, instead of the usual white and tan. It looked fresh. She stooped over it and sniffed. Rolf abandoned his toy for a moment, stuck his snout in close, and joined in. She couldn't help laughing. Like dog, like master. She smelled fresh tobacco smoke. She tagged the butt. There might be usable DNA on it, or if they were really lucky, it'd be some kind of exotic, rare brand of smokes.

"Camels, probably," she muttered. But she called another cop over to keep an eye on the parking spot until the CSU van arrived. Then she went back to the room.

"Find anything?" she asked, leaning through the window. Vic and Levine were still looking over the bodies.

"Yeah," Vic said. He had on gloves and was leafing through a nice-looking wallet. "The guy's got a driver's license, name of Gregory Markov. Credit cards, a couple hundred in cash, library card." He grinned sardonically. "Pics of the wife, too."

"Any kids?" Erin asked.

"No pics of them," he said. "Wedding ring's still on his finger. Nice watch. Not a Rolex, but classy."

"He carrying?" she asked.

"Nope," Vic said. "No weapon, not even a pocketknife. No cell phone, either, which is weird. Car keys. Toyota. Bet we find it in the lot, and a phone in the car."

"A Toyota?" she echoed. "No Mercedes? No Audi?"

"I know, crazy," Vic said. He pointed the key fob at the window and pushed one of the buttons. From Erin's right came the familiar chirp of a car door unlocking. Headlights blinked. She looked to see what it was.

"You've gotta be kidding me," she said. "It's a Prius."

"Not exactly a gangster-mobile," Vic said. "We'll need to check the car, of course."

"What about the girl?" she asked.

"No idea," Vic said. "No purse, no ID. All she's got is her clothes."

"Any idea who she might be?" Erin persisted.

"She's a pro," Vic said. "Dress like that, she's gotta be. And she looks like she's not a day over seventeen. Maybe younger. Might be in the system, might not. We'll check with Vice, run her prints. She's blond, pretty. Can't tell much else."

"Needle tracks on her arms," Levine put in. "She was a heroin user. But the marks aren't fresh. I'll run the bloodwork, but I'd guess she's been clean for a couple of weeks at least. No obvious tattoos. I'll look over her whole body for identifying marks. I'll do that back at the lab."

"Anything outside?" Vic asked. "I don't see you coming back with three gunmen in bracelets."

"I found where they stashed the getaway," she said. "One cigarette butt, some tire tracks, and maybe something they dropped in the storm drain on the way out."

"Better than nothing," he said.

Erin looked around the room. "What else can we do here?" she asked.

"CSU will dust for prints," Vic said. "And they'll look for body fluids, God help them. They'll collect all the physical evidence. Need any help with the stiffs?"

"Technically, you shouldn't call them stiffs until rigor mortis sets in," Levine said. "That usually takes two to six hours, starting with the face, neck, and jaw."

"Jesus," Vic said. "Sorry I asked. So what do I call them?"

"Victims?" Erin suggested.

"Right," he said. "Why don't we go see how the Lieutenant's getting on."

* * *

They found Webb and Jones in the lobby, having just finished talking to the night manager. The woman had calmed down a little, but she was still pretty obviously spooked. Her hands were shaking and she had a used tissue clenched in one fist. She kept tearing little bits of it off and scattering them on the floor.

Erin and Vic stepped outside with their colleagues and explained what they'd found. Webb listened, nodding.

"We don't have too much on our side," the Lieutenant said. "We know the shooting happened at quarter to ten, going by the lobby clock. According to Miss Walsh, there was no warning at all. No raised voices, just a lot of shooting, some screaming, then more shooting. She dove behind the counter, so she didn't see anything once holes started getting punched in the wall."

"Smart girl," Vic observed.

"She said there was a pause, maybe twenty seconds, but she's not sure about the timing. Then there was one more shot, and silence. She dialed 911, and while she was talking to Dispatch, she heard tires screech outside."

"She see the car?" Erin asked.

"Nope," Jones said. "She was still keeping her head down."

"That last shot sounds like the one into the girl's head," Erin said.

"That's what I'm thinking," Webb agreed.

"So no one got a look at the perps," Vic said. "Unless the camera's any good."

"We'll try it," Webb said. "But it was already dark out there. I'm guessing we get jack shit from it. We can at least confirm how many shooters."

"Does Miss Walsh remember anything about Markov and the girl?" Erin asked.

"Yeah," Jones said. "She says they came in separately, about fifteen minutes apart. The guy was first in. He paid for the room, cash, signed the register as Greg Marks."

"Fake name," Vic said. "Classy."

"The girl came in about twenty minutes before the shooting," Jones went on. "The witness says she was acting edgy, all twitchy and nervous. She asked for Greg's room. The manager told her which one it was, and she went down the hall."

"Huh," Vic said. "They must've set up the meeting ahead of time. Usually, the john comes in with the hooker, not one at a time. Maybe he was a regular for her."

"Did she have a purse with her?" Erin asked.

Jones shrugged. "I dunno. Manager didn't say."

"There wasn't a purse in the room," Webb said.

"Exactly," Erin said.

Webb snapped his fingers. "Just a minute." He went back to the lobby. A moment later he returned. "Clerk says she had a black purse, basic handbag."

"The shooters took her purse," Jones said.

"And left his wallet," Vic said. "Who robs a hooker and leaves the john's money?"

"Someone who knows hookers get paid in cash," Webb said.

"Twenty minutes," Erin said.

"What's that?" Webb asked.

"The two of them were alone for twenty minutes," Jones said. She'd followed Erin's line of thinking. "If they came to the motel to get it on, they were taking their sweet time. They still had all their clothes on when they were shot."

"Or they put them on again," Vic suggested.

Everyone looked at him.

He shrugged. "Twenty minutes is plenty of time."

Jones shook her head. "For you, maybe," she said. "A real man takes his time."

Webb snorted, and Erin had to bite back a laugh.

"We'll know from Levine's report whether the girl had sex," Webb said, before Vic said anything else. "No need to speculate. What I want to know is, how did the shooters know which room to target?"

"Did anyone else come through the lobby after the victims?" Erin asked.

"Miss Walsh says no," Jones said. "But she also took a bathroom break just after the girl arrived."

"We need to dust the register for prints," Webb said. "I'm

thinking one of them came into the lobby and looked up the room number. Nothing else makes sense, unless one of the victims told the shooters where they'd be."

Just then, a shout from the parking lot got their attention. One of the uniformed officers was running toward them.

"We've got a gun!" he yelled. "In the drain. Pistol."

Webb clenched his fist. "Great work, O'Reilly."

"It was Rolf," she said, rubbing her partner's head.

"Then tell him great work, from me," Webb said, hurrying toward the drain. The others followed.

The second cop, wearing gloves, was holding a pistol by the barrel. "It was right on top, in plain view once we popped the lid off," he said.

"What kind of gun is that?" Jones asked, squinting along her flashlight beam. "Doesn't look like one I've seen before."

"It's a Makarov," Vic said. "You don't see many of them in the US."

"Russian gun?" Erin guessed.

"Yeah," Vic said. "Soviet cops used them up through the Nineties. It's reliable, but its ballistics are worse than our nine-millimeters, and the ammo's incompatible. No wonder they threw it away. They'd have trouble getting reloads over here."

"What's a Russian handgun doing here?" Jones asked.

"I'll bet it's the one that shot the girl," Erin said.

The coroner's van had pulled up to the motel while they were talking.

"Oh, great," Vic said. "The meat wagon. I just know it's gonna be Hank and Ernie."

"Who're they?" Erin asked.

"They're the guys we hide when the press comes around," Jones said. "They're... well, you'll see."

Erin figured there had to be some sort of contract that required one tall, thin guy and one short, fat guy. In this case,

Ernie was the tall one and Hank was the short one. They were rolling their stretchers into the motel. As the detectives got there, they could hear Hank saying, "Well, no one can say they didn't go out with a bang."

"Y'know," Ernie replied, "One of the ESU guys told me firing a submachine-gun full auto is the closest a guy can come to having a multiple orgasm."

"Interplay of sex and violence," Hank agreed solemnly. "It's all over film, TV, you name it. Sex and death."

"Oh, for the love of God," Webb said. "Will you two shut the hell up? You're getting paid to move bodies, not exercise your jaws."

"That's what she said," Ernie said to his partner.

Erin blinked. "Did they really...?" she asked Jones in an undertone.

"Yeah," Jones said. "There's no excuse for them."

"We done here, sir?" Vic asked.

"Pretty much," Webb said. "We'll let the evidence techs work the place over. Let's look at Markov's car, then get back to the precinct."

"We don't want to hit this fresh in the morning?" Jones asked.

"Sorry, Detective," Webb said. "Am I interfering in your busy evening plans?"

Jones sighed. "No, sir."

"Guess we'll have to have that drink another night," Erin said to Vic.

"Who knows?" Vic replied. "A lot can happen before the sun comes up."

*   *   *

Gregory Markov's Prius was almost brand-new, dark blue

and freshly washed. There was no sign of it having been disturbed. The only interesting thing was a cell phone in the glove compartment. Webb carefully lifted it out and checked it.

"Three missed calls," he said. "All of them from a contact called Nat. We'll dump the SIM card back at the station."

"No guns," Vic said. He'd been going through the trunk. "No drugs. No diamonds."

"You sound disappointed," Erin said.

"If I could find something that tied him to being a gangster, this would make more sense," Vic said. "This is just some ordinary guy's car. What the hell is going on? Guys who drive Priuses don't get done like Pacino in *Scarface*."

"So bad guys aren't allowed to drive environmentally-friendly cars?" Jones asked.

"You know what I mean," Vic said. "I'm not seeing any sign this guy was in the life."

"CSU can take a look," Webb said. "But I'm thinking the car's a bust. Saddle up, everyone. We're going home."

"If only that were true," Jones said gloomily.

"Hey, the NYPD's a family," Vic said. "A big, happy, dysfunctional, heavily-armed family."

"You make us sound like the Corleones," Erin said. Vic had put Al Pacino movies on her mind.

"Lots of armed organizations pretend they run New York City," Vic pointed out. "We're the only ones that actually do."

Chapter 4

The first thing they did back at the precinct was start a fresh pot of coffee. Then they started hunting for information. Jones looked up Markov's record. Vic went down to the morgue to get a set of prints off the Jane Doe and run them. Webb and Erin were cataloging the evidence they'd recovered from the scene. While they were working, Markov's cell phone started ringing.

"Nat again," Erin said. "Persistent." She glanced at the clock, which read a little past two.

"Pick it up," Webb said. "Whoever it is, they don't know he's dead. Maybe we can get some info."

"Okay." Erin took a deep breath and answered. "Hello?"

There was a short, baffled pause. Then a woman's voice, heavily accented, said, "I am sorry, I must have wrong number."

"Is this Nat?" Erin asked, before the other woman could hang up.

There was another pause. "Yes. Who are you?"

"My name is Detective O'Reilly," Erin said. "NYPD. Please identify yourself, ma'am."

"I am Natalie Markov," the woman replied. She had sounded

confused. Now she sounded scared. "Why do you have Gregory's telephone? Is he all right?"

"Ma'am, are you at home right now?" Erin asked.

"Yes. Is Gregory okay? Please, you are scaring me." Natalie was getting more frantic.

"Ms. Markov, is Gregory Markov your husband?"

"Yes!" Natalie shouted. "Now tell me where he is!"

Erin closed her eyes. "We need to talk, Ms. Markov. Something's happened. We need you to come in to the station right away."

*   *   *

"I do not understand," Natalie said. "How could this happen?"

Natalie Markov was a tall, slender blonde in her early thirties. She was very pretty, crossing the line into beautiful. She had a model's face, high cheekbones, striking blue eyes, and a firm chin. She wasn't crying. She sat in front of Erin's desk, looking shell-shocked.

Webb should've been doing this, Erin thought bitterly. But rank had its privileges, and one of them was delegating the unpleasant parts of police work to underlings. "Why don't you and Jones talk to her," he'd said.

"Why us?" Erin asked.

"Because you'll do better at this sort of thing than I would," Webb had said. "You've got more natural empathy."

"He means it's an emotional thing, and chicks are better at that," Jones had whispered in Erin's ear, rolling her eyes.

So here they were, with New York City's newest widow. Natalie had arrived by taxi so quickly after their phone conversation that Erin was half-tempted to flag down the cabbie and give him a speeding ticket on general principle. They'd taken her to the morgue to ID the body, per departmental procedure, and Natalie had agreed that yes, the man on the slab was her husband. Now they were back upstairs. Natalie had a glass of water and a box of tissues on her side of Erin's desk, but hadn't touched them.

"Ma'am, we're very sorry for your loss," Erin said for the fourth or fifth time. "And we want to help you. Do you know anyone who might have wanted to hurt Gregory? Anyone at all?"

"No," Natalie said. "My husband is a good man. He helps people. He has no enemies."

"How long have you been married, Ms. Markov?" Jones asked.

"Five years."

"You have an accent, ma'am," Jones said. "Where are you from?"

"I was born in Saint Petersburg," Natalie said. "I moved here ten years ago."

"Is Gregory from Russia, too?" Erin asked.

"Yes," Natalie said. "His birth name is Grigori. When he came to America, he changed the spelling to Gregory, to better fit in."

"Did you meet in Russia?" Jones asked.

"No," Natalie said. "It is not easy for immigrants, coming to your country. Many men will take advantage of a young woman with no family. Gregory helped me to find work. Since he came to America the same way, he always wished to help others." Now, at last, there were tears in her eyes. "He was so kind to me."

"What line of business was your husband in?" Jones asked.

"Imports," she said. "Gemstones."

Erin and Jones exchanged a glance. Neither of them said *smuggler*. Jones made a note on her pad.

"Do you have any children, ma'am?" Erin asked.

Natalie shook her head. "No. We tried for several years. Last year, I became pregnant. But we lost the baby four months into the pregnancy."

"That must have been hard," Jones said. "How did he handle it?"

"He was very upset," Natalie said. "And he worried about me very much. We both wanted a child so badly."

Erin swallowed. This line of questions wasn't pleasant. "Was Gregory distant lately?" she asked. "Was he acting at all strange? Like maybe he was hiding something?"

"No," Natalie said. Then she hesitated. "He hinted there might be a surprise, for our anniversary. He said I would be very happy with it."

"Is it possible he might have been seeing another woman?" Erin asked.

"*Nevozmozhno!*" Natalie snapped. Seeing their blank looks, she shook her head violently. "Not possible! You are asking if Gregory had a girlfriend? No! We were happy to be married! We... we were... happy..." Her self-control crumbled as the reality of the situation finally sank in. She buried her head in her hands.

"Natalie," Erin said as gently as she could. "Is there any reason your husband would have been at a motel with a young woman?"

"What woman?" Natalie demanded. "Who has said this?"

"There was a woman found with him," Erin explained. "She was also killed."

Jones took out a photo from the morgue. Erin wished they had a live snapshot of the girl. But then, if they did, they might not need anyone to ID her.

"My God," Natalie whispered. "No, I do not know her. But if Gregory was with her, it is because he was wishing to help her. That is the man he is... the man he was."

* * *

"What've you got?" Webb asked.

"He was a great guy," Jones said dryly. "Everyone loved him. Pillar of the community. No enemies, no debts, no shady connections."

"Damn," Webb said.

Erin tried not to look as unhappy as she felt. They'd gotten nothing useful out of Natalie. Markov's widow had left after her interview was done, to make arrangements with his business and for the funeral. "Either he was a hell of an actor, or there's nothing he was hiding," she said. "Natalie... Ms. Markov... seemed genuine."

"You buy it?" Webb asked Jones.

She nodded. "Yeah. Natalie doesn't know jack about why he got killed."

Webb rubbed his temples. "Russians," he said.

"The Markovs came from Russia, sir," Erin said.

"Not what I meant, O'Reilly," he said. "Neshenko dropped by Evidence. The prints aren't in-system. But he was able to ID the cigarette butt you found."

"Yeah, it was a funny color," Erin said.

"Exactly. Apparently it's a Sobranie Black, a Russian brand."

"Can you get them in the States?" she asked.

"Yeah, unfortunately," Webb said. "They're available online, like every damn thing these days. But think about it. Russian cigs, Russian handgun in the drain, Russian victim in the morgue."

"Two Russian victims, if it turns out Jane Doe's from there, too," Erin pointed out.

"Yeah," Webb said. "And Markov was importing gems. Maybe he screwed someone over on a deal."

"The wife wouldn't necessarily know about that," Jones said. "Hell, maybe it was a legitimate deal from Markov's point of view, but he didn't know who he was messing with."

"Jones, I want you to start running Markov's financials," Webb said. "Then get in on the international jewel trade. Get a client list. I want to know who Markov was doing business with, and their street reps. See if anything pops."

"On it, sir," Jones said. She rolled her chair back behind her desk and set to work at her computer.

"What about me, sir?" Erin asked.

"I want you working on an ID of the other victim," Webb said. "Since you've got ten bucks riding on it, see if you can find out who she is and why anyone would want her dead bad enough to blow away another guy and half a motel room. Start down in the morgue, talk to Levine."

"I thought the prints came up blank," Erin said.

"Be creative, O'Reilly," Webb snapped. "Figure it out. It's three thirty in the morning, I have a headache, and I'm not gonna hold your hand on this. Do your job."

"Yes, sir," Erin said. It was the only thing she could say.

*   *   *

Levine was in the lab, looking into a microscope, when Erin came in.

"What can you tell me about the victim?" Erin asked.

"Which one?" Levine asked without looking up.

"The one we don't have identified," Erin said.

"Which one?" Levine repeated, still staring at the scope.

"There's just the two bodies," Erin said.

"Three," Levine corrected.

"Huh?"

Levine looked up then and blinked at Erin through her

glasses. "It depends on how you define victim," she said. "New York state law says there's only two."

"What the hell are you talking about?" Erin was exhausted, hopped up on late-night caffeine, and in no mood to play games.

"There isn't currently a state statute regarding murder of an unborn child," Levine said. "The Unborn Victims of Violence Act would classify this as an additional homicide, but only if it took place in federal jurisdiction, so maybe it just counts as two."

"Hold on," Erin said. "Just stop. Are you telling me Jane Doe was pregnant?"

"Yes," Levine said. "About halfway through the second trimester."

"Jesus." Erin took a step back and leaned against the wall. "Okay, we're going to need you to run the bloodwork on the fetus. The first thing we've got to know is whether Markov is the dad, obviously."

"I'm already checking the woman," Levine said. "No drugs in her system. She's a recovering addict, no doubt about it. The needle tracks aren't fresh. Noradrenaline levels are normal."

"What's that mean?" Erin asked. "Let's assume I don't have a medical degree."

"It means she's been clean for a few weeks at least," Levine explained. "The physiology returns to normal. The addictive behaviors take longer to correct, but she made it through the initial withdrawal period."

"Good for her," Erin said. "Maybe when she found out she was pregnant, she figured she had to kick the habit."

"It's possible," Levine said. "The effects of opioid abuse on unborn children can be extremely negative."

"Still doesn't tell us who she was," Erin said. "No match on the prints. I'm guessing nothing on dental records, either."

"She had some dental work done in a former Soviet-bloc

country," Levine said. "When she was a little girl."

"How do you know that?"

"Gold," Levine said. "Crowns and fillings in gold were very popular in Russia until just a few years ago. I'd guess she came from a smaller rural town, where dentistry hasn't caught up. They're using composite fillings, mostly, in Moscow these days."

"Levine," Erin said, "how do you get all this in your head?"

"I read a lot."

"Okay." Erin sighed. "So you know where she got her teeth done, sort of, but no American dental records. No identification at all. Just a pregnant girl, probably from Russia. Anything else you can tell me? Anything at all?"

"She was physically abused," Levine said.

"How? When?"

"There's fresh bruising over more faded marks. It's what I'd expect to see on a battered spouse, or a child from an abusive home. Mostly localized to the backs of the thighs and lower back. Judging from the marks, I'd guess an extension cord or some other kind of insulated cable."

Erin closed her eyes. "Systematic beatings."

Levine nodded. "There's also some bruising on the stomach and abdomen. I'm a little surprised it didn't induce a miscarriage."

"Any chance Markov inflicted any of the injuries?" Erin asked.

"Hard to say," Levine said. "The marks on the back and legs were too old to have been received tonight. She wasn't beaten this evening. But this might not be the first time they've met."

"Got anything else for me?"

"Not right now," the medical examiner said. "I have been able to determine the cause of death was definitely multiple gunshot wounds to both adults, with the pistol shot to the female victim's head inflicted at time of death. Markov was killed by the shots to his torso, almost instantly. It's likely she would have died from her other wounds before the paramedics arrived, regardless of the head GSW."

"Okay, thanks," Erin said. "Let us know what else you come up with."

As she waited for the elevator to take her back upstairs, Erin knew one thing at least. She was going to find out what had happened to that girl, and she was going to make the bastards pay for it.

Chapter 5

Webb finally called off the night's work at four. "Go on, everybody go home," he said. "Get some sleep, then get back in here."

Erin, in a fog of fatigue, leashed up Rolf. The dog, who'd been sleeping on his carpet square beside her desk, hopped to his feet, ready to go out and get back to work. They got in her car and started driving, a cup of coffee—her fifth of the night—in her hand so she wouldn't drive into the East River.

She was halfway to Queens when she remembered she didn't live in Queens anymore.

"Damn, damn, damn," she muttered. At least the bridge wasn't too busy this time of night. She had to go all the way across before she could turn around, though. Her first night of living in Manhattan wasn't off to a promising start.

Finally, she got to her new apartment. The bed wasn't made; she and Vic had just dropped it in the bedroom before hurrying off to the crime scene. She decided she didn't care. She stripped down to her underwear, threw on a loose T-shirt, tossed a pillow onto the bare mattress pad, and lost consciousness.

* * *

Sometimes all it took to crack a case was coming at it fresh, with a few hours of sleep. This wasn't one of those times. When Erin dragged herself out of bed at her usual wake-up time, having slept less than three hours, she was still tired, her apartment was still full of boxes of stuff, and she still had no idea who Jane Doe was.

She took Rolf for a jog, jumped into the shower while her coffee-maker worked its magic, fried a couple of eggs, downed a glass of orange juice, and took the coffee with her to the precinct. She got there twenty minutes early and realized she was still a little out of it. This living-in-the-city business was taking some getting used to.

The first thing she did was talk to the Vice squad. Sergeant Brown was head of the Vice unit at Precinct 8. He held an office in a converted supply closet, which meant it was poorly ventilated and had no windows. Brown himself was a bitter, cynical, heavyset cop with a very dim view of human nature. When Erin knocked on his door, he was looking at a magazine, his feet propped up on his desk.

"Morning, Detective," he said. "You're up early."

"Do you ever go home?" she asked. His office looked lived-in, with empty takeout containers, soda cans, and even a clothes bar on one side of the room with spare shirts hanging on it.

"Why would I want to go home? There's nothing I want to do there."

"Is there anything you want to do here?"

"Not really. But I'm already here, you see."

She leaned forward, squinting in the faint light of a fluorescent fixture with a bad ballast. "Are you looking at porn?"

He smiled sourly and tilted the cover of the magazine

toward her. Three women were on the cover, twisted into some sort of bizarre pretzel shape with big, fake smiles plastered on their faces. "Yep," he said. "I'm the only guy in this city who has to sneak the Wall Street Journal into his desk drawer, but can read skin mags in front of his coworkers. Afraid I can't let you have it; it's crime-scene collateral. But if you're interested, I got some other stuff. All shapes, sizes, positions, orientations."

"No thanks, I'm good," Erin said. "I was hoping you could help me with a homicide ID."

"Got a dead streetwalker?"

"Good guess."

"Most of them have priors," he said. "She'll probably be printed."

"She's not. We ran her prints first thing."

"Okay," Brown took his feet off his desk with a sigh. He popped open a can of Mountain Dew and took a swig. "What's her profile?"

"What do you want to know?" Erin asked.

He sighed again. "Whatever you got. We're saying 'she', so I'm guessing we're not talking rough trade, or a rent-boy dressed as a girl. How old?"

"Seventeen, maybe eighteen."

"Ethnic group?"

"White. Blonde, blue eyes."

Brown nodded. "Drug use?"

"Heroin tracks, but bloodwork says she's been clean for a few weeks. The drugs tell you anything?"

Brown shrugged. "Everyone's addicted to something."

"Everyone?"

"Not just drugs," he said. "Some people are sex addicts, some are food addicts. You're addicted, I'm addicted. It's how we're wired. It's biological."

"Bullshit."

"How much coffee you drink?"

Erin didn't answer.

"How much time off you take?" he went on.

"That's not what we're talking about."

"Of course it is. Our whole job in Vice is busting the addicts our society's decided are addicted to the wrong stuff. Hookers, blow, kiddie porn. Fast foot, coffee, and working on weekends are fine. Boffing the secretary's borderline, but you usually get away with it."

Erin shook her head. "How do you even get up in the morning?"

He smiled wearily. "I'm an addict, too. I'm the guy who slows down when he passes a bad highway crash. Just can't look away from the way New Yorkers fuck up their lives. Now, this working girl of yours, she have any scars, tattoos, other marks?"

"No ink," Erin said. "She'd been beaten systematically, over a period of time. And she was pregnant."

"That explains kicking the needle habit," Brown said. "I'm surprised she had the willpower. I'm even more surprised her pimp let her off the chemical leash."

Erin hadn't thought about that. Now, hearing the Vice cop say it, she realized it made sense. Lots of pimps used drugs to control their girls, keeping them dependent and compliant. Jane Doe might not have had a choice about taking drugs. How had she managed to stay clean? Heroin had really obvious withdrawal symptoms. Her pimp would've known she was trying to get off the stuff.

"Maybe she was on the run," Erin said. "Got out of a bad situation?"

"Sounds like she was trying to get out of the life," Brown suggested. "It happens. Some of them even make it, but if they've got no one to go to, most are back turning tricks inside two months."

"Maybe she did have someone to go to," Erin said, thinking of what Natalie Markov had said about her husband. "She was killed when she was with a guy with a rep for helping down-and-out immigrants."

"She from overseas?" Brown asked.

"We think so," Erin said. "She had some dental work like you'd get in Russia eight or ten years ago."

"Okay," Brown said. "I don't know who she was, but I can tell you what she was. Human trafficking. Jesus, I hate that term. Sounds like we're handing out parking tickets. Pretty teenager gets grabbed by Russian Mafia goons, they fill her head with promises about the great life in America, or maybe it's just straight-up kidnapping. They ship her over, fill her with drugs, beat her till she knows who's in charge, then have her make money for them on her back till she gets used up and kicks off."

Erin nodded. "You're probably right. You think she came here illegally?"

"I'd bet my shield on it. That way they can threaten her with deportation, too."

"If she was kidnapped, why the hell would she be scared of being sent home?"

"You have any idea what it's like over there?" Brown retorted. "You want to understand Russia? Think of it like this. They're the people who put up with the Communists because the Commies were better than the Czars. Russia's a pit, O'Reilly, just like the human soul. It's big, it's black, and believe me, there is no bottom."

"Brown," Erin said, "if I ever feel like I'm not taking my work seriously enough, I'll come talk to you for a half-hour or so."

"Glad to help."

"So how do I find who this girl was?"

"You find who she worked for," Brown said.

"I was kind of hoping to use her to find who she was

working for, not the other way round," Erin said.

"I don't mean talk to the pimp," he said. "Those Russian Mafia are serious sons of bitches. They're the guys who wouldn't talk when the KGB went at them with the pliers. The stuff we're allowed to do in this great country of ours won't even tickle 'em. No, you gotta find one of her coworkers."

"So I should start chatting up hookers?"

Brown snorted. "You have any idea how many streetwalkers we've got in this city?"

"No."

"Neither does anyone else," Brown said. "There's about a million in the USA, give or take. That's one for every three hundred people. They pull in about fourteen billion dollars a year. If they incorporated, they'd be Fortune 500."

"I need an in," Erin said.

"You need an in," he agreed. "A CI. You got anyone you can lean on?"

"Not really," she admitted. "I haven't got a network built up yet."

"I'll ask around," he said. "But don't hold your breath. There's too many girls like the one you've got on your desk."

"Okay," Erin said. "Thanks anyway."

"Don't mention it," Brown said. "You need anything else, don't hesitate to ask. After all, that's what Vice is all about. Whatever you want, we know how to get it for you."

She rolled her eyes and got the hell out of there.

Chapter 6

Vic and Jones were at their desks when Erin and Rolf walked in. Vic was chewing a toothpick and scowling at his computer. He was twirling something in his fingers. At first she thought it was a pen.

"What's up?" Erin asked.

He tossed the small, dark cylinder to her. She caught it and saw it was black, with a gold filter. "Sobranie Black?" she guessed.

"Yeah," he said. "Picked it up on the way in."

"Not as rare as we were hoping?"

Vic snorted. "Rare? Bought it off a newsstand in Little Odessa. Any Russian neighborhood has 'em."

"But it is a Russian import," Jones said. "I'd never heard of them until last night. These have got to be Russians."

"They're your people, right?" Erin said to Vic. "You think we've got a chance of finding them?"

He gave her a flat stare. "Christ. You think there's America, and then all the other countries are these little places where everyone knows each other? Russia's the biggest country in the world. Eleven time zones. Eleven. Anyway, I was born here. I'm a New Yorker."

"Okay, okay," Erin said. "I'm just thinking you might know some things about Russian immigrants."

He sighed. "Yeah, I've been thinking about it all night. I can ask around the old neighborhood, see if anyone's talking, but don't get your hopes up. It's just like the Italians back in the '40s. They're a lot more scared of the gangsters than they are of anyone else. No one's gonna say anything, not to you, not to me."

"We need a CI," Erin said, thinking what Brown had said. "Someone who'll get us insider info."

"Good luck with that," Vic said. "These guys are probably Russian Mafia. They find out there's a snitch, the biggest piece of him you'll find will be his tongue, and you'll only find that 'cause they'll mail it to you."

Erin made a face. "You need another cup of coffee. That'll cheer you up."

"I don't want to be cheered up," he growled. "I want to find these sons of bitches. I checked gun registries, just in case. The Makarov isn't registered, of course."

"The girl was pregnant," Erin said.

"Really?" Jones looked up. "Damn."

"Yeah," Erin said. "Who do you think the dad is?"

"What's it matter?" Vic retorted. "What it's worth, I'm betting it's Markov. But it could be any of her Johns."

"Yeah, maybe," Erin said, unconvinced. She sat down at her own desk and logged on to her computer. Rolf settled onto his carpet square beside her.

"So, the Fourth's coming up next week," Jones said after a few minutes. "Anyone got big plans? Setting off some fireworks?"

"I used to love the Fourth of July," Vic said. "Then I became a cop. Explosives plus alcohol. Fun times for New York's finest. I just hope no drunken assholes blow up their houses this year."

"How about you, Erin?" Jones asked.

"I'm going up to my mom and dad's," she said. "Dad bought a place upstate after he retired. Hunting in the winter, fishing in the summer. He always said he wanted to get out of the city. My whole family's going to be there."

"How many of you are there?" Jones asked.

Erin counted them off on her fingers. "Three brothers. Sean Junior, Michael, and my kid brother Tommy. Sean's married to Michelle, two kids, Anna and Patrick. Michael's married to Sarah, no kids yet. Tommy's... well, Tommy's got a guitar."

"Wow," Jones said. "Irish Catholic, huh? I'll be hanging with my mom, just the two of us."

"What about the Lieutenant?" Erin asked.

"What about him?" Webb asked, coming into the office. "You're all here. Good. I hope you're not making big holiday plans. We've still got a case to crack."

"You know, sir," Jones said, "recent research shows that a forty-hour week is actually less productive than a four-day week. Working long hours erodes efficiency."

"That so?" Webb said. "Forty-hour weeks. God, the private sector. I wish I had forty-hour weeks."

"Nine to five," Jones said wistfully. "But what would we do with all that free time?"

"I was thinking," Vic said. "Maybe I'll go out tonight, grab a beer, pick up a hooker."

Jones shook her head. "You're worse than the dog. At least he's housebroken."

"Leave Rolf out of this," Erin said.

"I'll expense the hooker to the department," Vic went on.

"Jesus, you sound like you're serious," Jones said.

Erin got it. "You're gonna troll Little Odessa, talk to some of the street girls, see if you can find one who knows our victim."

"You got a better idea?" Vic asked.

"I'll keep grinding on Markov," Jones said. "I don't care how clean he looks. Everybody's hiding something."

"This job will make you cynical," Webb observed. "Ten more years and you'll be just like me."

"God, I hope not," Jones said. "I don't ever want to look that bad in a trench coat."

Webb gave her a sarcastic smile that barely twitched one corner of his mouth. "Okay, enough grab-ass. Back to work."

* * *

The word Jones had used was "grinding," and that was what they did. Erin went through hundreds of mug shots and Vice prostitution reports, hoping to find something that would lead to the Jane Doe. She got nothing. There were just too many teenage hookers in New York, and more coming in all the time. The only useful conclusion she came to was a negative one. If the victim had been in town more than a few months, she'd probably have some sort of record, so the absence of information suggested she was a relative newcomer. That didn't help if she'd been brought in illegally, which was almost certainly true. That way her pimp could threaten her with deportation along with her heroin dependency and the physical intimidation. This girl hadn't had a chance.

Vic stayed on the phone most of the day, talking in Russian. Judging from the length of the conversations, and the way he kept pounding his fist into his desk between calls, he got hung up on a lot.

Jones, despite her guarantee that everyone had secrets, had to admit that Gregory Markov just might be clean. "No mob connections at all," she said. "Never arrested. If it wasn't for the INS, we wouldn't even have had his prints on file. Just married the once. No drugs, no domestic abuse. Uniforms never got called to his house. I don't believe it. How's a guy like that get mowed down?"

"Same way everyone else does," Webb said. "Bullets aren't like Santa Claus. They don't care if you've been naughty or nice."

"Wait a second," Jones said. She'd been leaning back in her chair, stretching. Now she sat forward.

Everyone looked her way. "What've you got?" Erin asked.

"Something weird," Jones said. "I've got Markov's bank records here. I was looking for extra money coming in, money laundering, drugs, that sort of thing. Nothing popped."

"So?" Webb said.

"So there's nothing like that," she said. "But there's money going out."

"What do you mean?" Erin asked, coming over to stand behind Jones's chair. She was still a beat cop at heart. Struggling through her own income tax returns was the best she could do at accounting.

"I mean Markov's got cash withdrawals," Jones said. "Sizable ones. And they're regular. Look, about five thousand a month. Always in cash."

"Gambling problem?" Vic guessed.

"Blackmail payouts?" Webb suggested.

Jones shrugged. "How do I know? Maybe he got in deep to loan sharks and they gunned him."

"No," Erin said. "You owe a Shylock, he doesn't kill you. Besides, Markov had plenty of money."

"No kidding," Jones said. "He kept a healthy balance all the time. You think the wife knew about this?"

"Try this for size," Webb said. "Markov's banging nice, young teenage tail, fresh from Mother Russia. But he knocks up this one girl, and she starts blackmailing him. Maybe she keeps the cash, maybe she hands it on to her pimp. Anyway, he pays so the wife doesn't find out. But she does find out. And she gets pissed."

"So she hires a Russian death squad to gun both of them?" Vic said. "I dunno."

"If it was a crime of passion, she'd probably kill him herself," Erin said.

"Maybe she did," Webb said. "She's from Russia, maybe she knows some tough guys from over there. We don't know she wasn't at the scene."

Erin thought about Natalie Markov. She somehow couldn't see the woman spraying submachine-gun fire into a motel room. But it wasn't like she had any better ideas. "How long till we get the DNA back on the baby?" she asked.

Webb sighed. "This isn't TV, O'Reilly," he said. "Last I checked, the DNA lab was three months backlogged. On important cases. We'll get the results in time for the trial. Maybe."

"Levine can at least get us a blood type," Erin said. "If it doesn't match, that would eliminate Markov as the father."

"Which leaves us nowhere," Vic said gloomily. "Like we were before. Picking up teenage hookers is sounding better and better."

"You want me to come with?" Erin asked.

"You've gotta be shitting me," Vic said. "A guy like me, sure, maybe I could be looking for some action. The two of us together, we might as well put on our dress blues, throw our hats in the air, and sing 'New York, New York.'"

"Okay, Neshenko," Webb said. "Go out there, see what you can find. But watch your step. These are serious players. Have a piece on you, and make sure backup's in the area."

"If I'm extra-special good, can I stay up half an hour past my bedtime?" Vic asked.

"Knock it off," Webb said. "I ask for a detective squad, I get standup comedians."

There wasn't much to laugh about. They only had one real lead to follow, and that was the money from Markov's accounts. It was pretty thin.

"He might be laundering money for the Russian mob," Jones said. "But I doubt it."

"How can you tell?" Erin asked.

"The income looks legit," Jones said. "The withdrawals are sloppy by comparison. If this guy was a professional, he'd have disguised the outflow better. And there's just not enough of it. Mob money launderers move lots of money, seven, eight figures. Our boy's shifting what, five K a month? That's nothing."

"People get killed over less," Erin said.

"But not mobsters," Webb said. "What's his highest account balance?"

Jones glanced through Markov's bank record. "Forty grand. His jewelry business account carries higher balances, mid six figures, but nothing out of the ordinary on it. I'm still double-checking some of the transactions, but it looks clean."

"Why don't we ask the wife?" Erin asked.

"You think she knows about it?" Vic replied.

"That's why I want to ask her," Erin shot back.

"Okay, go for it," Webb said.

"I'll keep going over the business records," Jones said. "See if I missed anything."

Erin dialed Natalie's number. The Russian woman picked up on the third ring.

"Yes?" Natalie said, sounding very tired.

"Hello, Ms. Markov, this is Erin O'Reilly, with the NYPD," Erin said, reflecting that death in America meant a lot of phone calls for the survivors. "I'm sorry to bother you, ma'am, but I was hoping I could talk to you a little about your husband."

Natalie hesitated. Then she cleared her throat and spoke firmly and clearly. "If it will help you to find who has done this terrible thing to Gregory, I will do everything I can. Do you have the address?"

"Yes, ma'am," Erin said. She'd gotten it from Markov's driver's license.

"Then you will come at once," Natalie said, more order than invitation.

"Thank you, Ms. Markov," Erin said. "I'll be there as soon as I can." She clipped on Rolf's leash and headed to her car. She caught up with Vic on the way. "You heading to Little Odessa?"

"Yeah," he said. "But we ought to go separate. I don't know how long I'm gonna be."

"I won't wait up for you."

*   *   *

The Markovs lived in Brighton Beach, an enclave at the southern tip of Brooklyn which had the largest population of Russian immigrants in the Western hemisphere. Erin took 478 through the Brooklyn-Battery Tunnel under the East River, then Ocean Parkway the rest of the way. She wasn't in a rush, which was good. The drive took 45 minutes. All the way down, she thought the case over. She didn't have enough pieces. They not only didn't have any suspects, they still didn't even know who one of the victims was.

"Maybe Markov knew her," she said to Rolf. "Hell, maybe she wasn't a call girl. Maybe she was out of the life. What do you think?"

Rolf didn't have an opinion.

Brighton Beach had been hit hard by a hurricane the previous summer, and Erin could see signs of damage. But the neighborhood was as busy as any in Brooklyn. She rolled down her window out of old Patrol habit as she drove through the streets, trying to get a sense of the local atmosphere and maybe catch something out of place. She heard as much Russian as English from the pedestrians.

The Markovs lived in a brick building near the beach. She parked in a police zone near the apartment, got Rolf out of the car, flipped her shield at the doorman, and went in.

Natalie answered the door immediately. She obviously hadn't slept much, if at all, judging by the dark shadows under her eyes. They went with her black silk blouse and skirt. She was very polite; her voice was calm and collected, with a heavy Russian accent.

"Come in, Officer O'Reilly," she said. "The water is ready. I will pour you some tea."

"Thank you, ma'am," Erin said, glancing around. It was a very nice apartment, spacious by New York standards, especially for a childless couple. The ceilings were a little low, but the place was clean and well-furnished.

"Please, make yourself comfortable," Natalie said, gesturing to a couch in the living room. "My home is yours."

"Thank you," she said again. While Natalie went into the kitchen, Erin took the opportunity to look around the room. There was a bookshelf full of books with a mix of English and Cyrillic titles. The mantelpiece had photographs of a serious-looking older couple, probably Natalie or Gregory's parents, a wedding picture of the two of them, and a photo of a Russian city, probably St. Petersburg.

The smell of tobacco hung in the air. An ashtray sat on the coffee table with a butt that was still smoking. Erin saw it was black with a gold filter.

"I am sorry," Natalie said as Erin was bending over to examine the ashtray. "It is a terrible habit, I know, but those are the most difficult to break."

Erin straightened up. She turned to the Russian woman, who brought in a tray with a teapot, sugar and cream bowls, two teacups, and a plate of shortbread cookies.

"How do you take your tea?" Natalie asked.

"Cream, no sugar, please," Erin said, deciding to try it the same way she had her coffee. She wasn't a tea drinker.

Natalie poured two cups and sat down in the armchair at the end of the table. Erin sat on the couch. Rolf settled himself at Erin's feet.

Natalie took out a black cigarette and a lighter. "Do you mind?"

Erin shook her head, knowing anything that relaxed Natalie would help with the interview. "Is that a Sobranie Black?" she asked.

"Yes," Natalie said, surprised. "You know it? I did not think anyone not Russian knows this brand." She lit the cigarette, settled it between her fingers, and took a long drag. "I told Gregory I would quit, but this has been a difficult twenty-four hours. I do not think he would mind."

Erin took a sip of tea. It was dark, strong, and bitter. "Ms. Markov, we've been going over your husband's information," she said. "We've been trying to figure out who would want to harm him. Did Gregory owe money to anyone?"

"No one," Natalie said.

"You're certain of that, ma'am?" Erin pressed. "Maybe a short-term loan, to cover an investment?"

"Certainly not," the other woman said, her eyes flashing. "Gregory always paid his debts."

"Do you know who he was paying each month?"

"What do you mean?"

"Five thousand dollars, cash, every month. Who was getting that money?"

Natalie said nothing.

"Ms. Markov," Erin said, leaning forward and putting her cup and saucer on the table. "You said you wanted to help me find your husband's killer. I need you to tell me the truth."

"It is not mine to tell," Natalie said.

Erin blinked. It was her turn to say, "What do you mean?"

"I will help you," Natalie said. "But there are others who might be hurt by this. How do I know they will be all right?"

"These others," Erin said. "Are they criminals?"

"Criminals!" Natalie said scornfully. "That word means so many things. In this country, you are a criminal if you kill a man, yes? But you are also a criminal if you smoke a cigarette with marijuana instead of tobacco. You are a criminal if you make a mistake on your taxes. You are a criminal if you do not have the correct permits to do business. You are a criminal if you come to this country without proper paperwork. It is just like under the Communists, except they made it a crime to leave and you make it a crime to come."

Erin understood. "If this is something to do with the INS," she said, "I'm not interested in that. I'm an NYPD Major Crimes detective, Ms. Markov. I'm not going to deport anybody. Was your husband helping illegal immigrants?"

"He did not hide money," Natalie said. "He did not even take a deduction on his taxes for this. He broke no laws."

Erin wasn't sure about that, but she wasn't an immigration lawyer. "How did he find the people who needed his help?" she asked.

"Gregory knew everyone in the importing business," Natalie said. "Some of them know people who bring other people on boats. They are poor. They pay more than they have just to come here." Natalie leaned across the table and laid her hand on Erin's. "There is so little opportunity in Russia, Officer O'Reilly. Many of these people are no more than children. Little girls with no money who do not speak the language. What becomes of them, once they are here?"

"Oh my God," Erin said quietly. "He was looking for

prostitutes. Just not for the reason we thought."

"My husband would never take advantage of a girl in such a position," Natalie said proudly. "He wished only to help them."

"Ms. Markov," Erin said. "This is important. Do you know who was running the girls?"

"I do not understand."

"I mean, when girls get brought in to be hookers, who brings them in? Do you know any names? Places?"

Natalie shook her head. "Gregory knew these things. He did not tell me."

"Did he have anything written down?" Erin asked. "Names, addresses, anything at all?"

"I do not know. I will look through his papers," Natalie said. "Do you think this is why Gregory was killed?"

"I don't know," Erin said. "But I'm going to find out."

Chapter 7

"Dead ends," Erin said, slamming the door of her apartment. "Nothing but dead goddamn ends."

Rolf wagged his tail. He wasn't ready to give up.

Erin smiled at her partner. "You did your part," she said. "We get the guy, maybe we get a DNA match from the cigarette in the parking lot. But it won't help us if he's not already in the database." She thought it over. "Shit. I should've got one of Natalie's butts out of the ashtray."

Rolf cocked his head.

"No, I don't think she did it," Erin said. "But we could at least run a match." She sighed. "We're done for the day. I'm gonna take a shower, and we're not gonna think about this any more tonight."

The German shepherd laid his snout between his paws and stared up at her.

"Yes, I'll feed you first," she said, getting out the kibble.

In spite of what she'd just said, she kept thinking while she stood under the showerhead. The hot water felt good on her neck and shoulders. They had no suspects. Her best guess was that Jane Doe's pimp had gotten a lead on her and followed her.

But why gun her down with a bystander present? What if Markov had pissed off the wrong guys and he'd been the target? What if the girl...

"Maybe she was bait," Erin said aloud. That was a thought. "Human traffickers, sick of easy marks getting scooped off the streets, lay out some bait for the good Samaritan. Markov can't resist, he goes for it, wants to talk to the girl. But the girl doesn't know the whole plan, or else they just don't give a damn and gun her along with him. Get rid of all the witnesses?"

She thought it over. "No," she said. "Girls are worth money to guys like that. No point in killing her if she's playing along. Hell, maybe she's got nothing to do with this, and she's just in the wrong place, wrong time, like all the rest of her life. Plain old shitty luck."

She was going in circles. She shut off the water and toweled off, then put on a long T-shirt over her underwear. By the time she'd gotten home from work, walked the dog, and cleaned up, it was too late and she was too tired to do anything else. An evening of mindless TV sounded about right.

She was midway through a rerun of "24" when her door buzzer went off, jolting her off the couch and onto her feet. Rolf jumped up, ears perked, ready for action.

"Yeah? Who is it?" she asked, punching the intercom button.

"It's Vic."

"Okay, sure. Come on up," she said, but she was a little confused. A glance at the clock told her it was later than she'd thought, almost ten. Then she looked at herself. "Pants," she said, grabbing a pair of sweats from the bedroom. She considered trying to dress up a little more, then decided the hell with it. She and Vic had been in a gunfight together. He could see her in comfy clothes. But she did add another layer, putting on a tank top and tossing the T-shirt back on top of it.

She was just in time. Vic knocked on the door as she poked her arms through the sleeves. She shook her hair back, double-checked the peephole just to be on the safe side, and opened the door.

"Evening," she said. "C'mon in."

"I didn't wake you up, did I?" Vic said, taking in her disheveled appearance.

"No," Erin said. "I'm just watching Jack Bauer beating up terrorists."

"Classic."

"Vic," Erin said.

"Yeah?"

"What are you doing here?"

"Oh," he said, looking at her. "Right now I was thinking, maybe I could take you up on that drink you were gonna get me."

"Vic, it's a work night," she said.

"I know. Look, we don't have to go anywhere fancy. I just want to talk."

"How'd you even know I'd be home?"

"I didn't."

"Vic, we've got these inventions, they're called phones." She looked more closely at him. "Are you okay?"

"Yeah. Absolutely." But he was distracted, edgy. He always had a restless energy to him, but at that moment, he couldn't stand still. He was pacing in the entryway, clenching and unclenching his hands.

"Okay," Erin said. "Let's get that drink. Maybe it'll settle you down. You're making me twitchy. Stay there. I'll put on something else. I didn't know I was stepping out tonight."

She changed into slacks and a blouse and pulled her hair into a ponytail. While she was doing it, another thought hit her. Not a pleasant one.

"Look, Vic," she said, coming out of the bedroom. "I don't want you getting the wrong idea here. You're my coworker and my friend, but—"

"Shit," he said. "I'm not asking you out, okay?"

"Okay, good."

"Good?" He sounded a little hurt.

"That's not what I meant," she said. "I mean, I don't like you."

"Good," he said more firmly. "I don't like you either."

"You're a jackass thug."

"And you're a hardass bitch."

"Glad we got that settled."

"Damn right. Now, we getting that drink?"

"Absolutely."

"Where's a good place around here?" Vic asked.

"I haven't had a chance to check out the neighborhood yet," Erin said. "There's... shit, the closest place is the Barley Corner. It's just two blocks that-a-way."

"Jesus Christ," Vic said. "That's the bar you almost blew up last time you were in it."

"Yeah," she admitted. "But it wasn't exactly me—"

"The one that's full of Irish mobsters," he continued.

"Right. Maybe somewhere else?"

"Maybe somewhere else," he agreed.

With the aid of Erin's smartphone, they found another joint a little further away, a bar called Last Call. It didn't have the class of the Corner, but it probably wasn't full of gangsters, either, so it seemed like a good compromise. They went in and got a table along the wall.

"What'll it be?" asked a tired-looking young woman with stringy hair.

"White Russian," Vic said.

"Two," Erin said. She wasn't much on vodka usually, but she

was always willing to try a different drink. Coffee liqueur sounded good, and it might sharpen her up a little.

She waited until the drinks arrived. Vic took a heavy slug of his. Erin sampled hers more carefully. She didn't know how strong it was, and wanted to take her time. "So, what's up?" she asked. "Is this about the case?"

"No," Vic said. "Well, maybe a little. Not really." He swirled his drink, staring at the patterns in the old fashioned cut glass.

Erin waited. This was good interrogation practice for her.

"I didn't find anything," he said. "Not about the victims. I guess I'm looking for advice."

"You? Advice?" She couldn't believe it. "Vic, how long have you been on the force?"

"Thirteen years."

"And you've been a detective longer than I have."

"Not that kind of advice," he said. "I'm talking about girl stuff."

"Girl stuff?" Erin echoed. "Oh, God. Talk to your mom about this. See, there's differences between boys and girls..."

Vic snorted. "That's not it either," he said. "Okay, I met this girl. Woman. Whatever. I was done knocking on doors, came up totally blank. Nobody talking. And I ran into her."

"What kind of girl? Streetwalker?"

"What? No!" Vic exclaimed. "What's the matter with you? No, she's just this girl, okay?"

"Okay," Erin said. "So what's special about her?"

"I talked to her."

"Yeah? And?"

"For three hours."

"What about it?"

"I've never talked to a girl for three hours," Vic said. "I don't like talking."

Erin smiled. "I've noticed," she said. "You'd rather be kicking down doors." Vic had been with the NYPD's ESU, Emergency Services Unit, doing SWAT-type work, before transferring to Major Crimes.

"Exactly," Vic said. "But she was interested in me. She was asking me questions, like she really wanted to get to know me."

"You think she was hitting on you?"

"Yeah."

"So what's the problem? She not your type?"

"She's exactly my type," Vic said. "And we had fantastic chemistry. I mean, I'm talking serious sparks."

"So why are you here, talking to your coworker, instead of getting it on in the backseat? Or did you already do the deed, and it was over too soon?"

"No," he said. "That's the thing. She wanted to, I'm sure of it. But she backed out."

"So that's what you want advice about," Erin said, taking another sip of her drink. "You want to understand the female psyche."

"Yeah."

"You may think this is strange, Vic," she said, unable to resist tweaking him a little. "But not every girl jumps in the sack with some guy she just met. You think she wants to see you again?"

"Yeah. She asked for my number."

"You give it to her?"

"Nine-one-one."

She laughed. "Seriously?"

"Okay, yeah, I gave her my number," Vic said. "I'm just trying to figure if it was a brushoff, or what. It was kinda strange."

"You get her digits?"

"No," he sighed. "Not even her last name."

"What's her first name?"

"Tatiana."

"Russian girl?"

"Yeah," Vic said. "And I'm a Russian guy. Match made in heaven."

"Well, you want my advice, so here it is," Erin said. "She got your number, and didn't give you hers. So she wants to be in the driver's seat. Let her. It's not like you've got a choice, right? Let her call you. If she does, you'll know she's interested. If not? You're screwed, and the hell with her."

"You're right," Vic said. He threw back the rest of his White Russian. "I didn't really need you to tell me that."

"I'm not a relationship counselor," she said. "I live with my dog, okay? You want to talk to a woman who's good at relationships, try my sister-in-law, Mrs. Happily Married."

"Nah," he said. "I just wasn't ready to go home yet. Still awake. Hell, maybe I'll drive back down to Little Odessa, pick up some whores."

"The way you say that really gives me the creeps," Erin said. "Wait a sec. You drove all the way up here to have one drink with me, and now you're gonna drive all the way back to south Brooklyn?"

"Line of duty, O'Reilly," Vic said. "Line of duty. And hey, you owed me a drink."

"You okay to drive?" she asked.

"Erin, I've had one," Vic said. "A Russian needs one drink just to deal with the existential pain of being Russian. We don't start to feel it till the third or fourth round."

"I guess the Irish are the same way," she said. "Be careful out there."

"Why's everybody keep telling me that?" he wondered.

Chapter 8

One of the most frustrating parts of detective work was waiting for things to happen. Lab results, paperwork, inquiries. Erin didn't like waiting. She liked doing. And what she was doing for the next few days, unfortunately, was nothing.

Vic was trying to make street-level contacts in Little Odessa and, Erin suspected, exploring the possibility of having a girlfriend. Jones was working the numbers at her computer, trying to find something—anything—that would provide a solid motive. Webb re-interviewed the night manager at the motel and anyone else connected to the case, which wasn't many people. He spent a lot of time on the phone with the Brighton Beach Vice squad, and almost as much time bitching about how unhelpful they were.

And Erin had no leads. It got so bad she actually started missing patrol duty. At least interesting things happened on patrol, even if those things involved drunken assholes throwing up in the back of her squad car. She and Rolf were both itching for action. She spun wheels for three days, drinking too much coffee, training with her K-9, and trying to think. The weekend came and went. Finally, Webb called her over to his desk.

"O'Reilly?"

"Yes, sir?"

"You getting anywhere?"

"No, sir."

"It's the Fourth on Thursday," he said. "You planning on seeing family?"

"If I'm needed here, I can let them know," she said, looking straight ahead.

"Come off it," Webb said. He sat back in his chair and rubbed his temples. "You know as well as I do that we're going nowhere. Your folks live upstate, right?"

"Yes, sir."

"Get out of town. Go see Mom and Dad. Come back fresh. If you head out Wednesday evening, can you be back at work Friday?"

"Sure thing," she said. Her heart leaped. She'd just about resigned herself to being alone on the holiday.

"You know what our homicide closure rate is?" he asked.

"Not exactly, sir."

"Rhetorical, O'Reilly," Webb said. "Last year it was seventy-four point eight percent, including cold cases. Not counting the cold ones, we cleared fifty-seven percent. It's basically a coin toss, and sometimes the coin comes up tails." He sighed. "And this one counts double. You know, it might have been out-of-town talent. In that case, we won't solve this one in a hurry, if at all."

"Yes, sir," Erin said, unable to think of anything else to say.

*   *   *

So she loaded Rolf into the Charger on Wednesday after work and headed to West Hurley, New York. It was a two-hour drive, which wasn't too bad. West Hurley was a town of about two thousand, set on the Ashokan Reservoir and surrounded by forest. Erin's dad had always said he'd get as far away from the city as he could when he retired from the NYPD, but no one had expected him to actually go through with it. Erin's mom hadn't wanted to be too far from her kids, so they'd compromised by staying in New York state, but getting well clear of the five boroughs.

Erin was a city girl. In fact, not counting New Jersey—and no self-respecting New Yorker would—she'd never been outside her home state. Now, driving out of Yonkers on 87, her mind cleared, but she also felt exposed.

There was still daylight when she drove into West Hurley. It was funny; Erin hadn't met anyone in New York City who'd ever heard of the town, but it was right next door to Woodstock, a place everyone knew. Erin's dad liked to point out that the famous music festival hadn't actually happened in Woodstock, but sixty miles southwest in Bethel. He didn't want people to think he was a Hippy.

Erin pulled into the driveway of her parents' house around sunset. Before she'd even shut off the engine, the front door was open. She stood up just in time to catch her niece Anna, a seven-year-old bundle of delighted energy, as the girl hurled herself into her arms.

"Guess what? I've decided to be a police officer, just like you and Grandpa!" Anna exclaimed, launching straight into conversation without bothering with a greeting.

"I thought you wanted to be a ballerina," Erin said.

"I'm going to do that, too," Anna said. "I'll dance when I'm not being a cop." She looked past Erin. "Rolfie!"

Erin set Anna down and let Rolf out of the back. She was lucky; Rolf was one of those police dogs who knew when they were off-duty. He treated children with gentle tolerance. The German shepherd nosed Anna in a dignified manner. The girl responded by flinging her arms around the dog's neck and vigorously hugging him.

"Great to see you again, Sis," said Michelle, Erin's sister-in-law. She'd come out onto the porch while Erin was dealing with Anna. Patrick, her other child, was five and a lot shyer. He lurked behind Michelle's legs, peering suspiciously at Erin.

Michelle had been married a decade to Erin's oldest brother, Sean Junior. She was a striking-looking woman in her upper thirties, a tall French-Canadian who'd somehow held onto her figure through two pregnancies and seven years of motherhood. She was also one of the friendliest, most positive people Erin had ever known.

"Hey, Shelly," Erin said. They embraced, and Michelle gave Erin a kiss on the cheek.

"C'mon inside," Michelle said. "Everyone else is here already. Did you have dinner?"

"Yeah, I ate on the way," Erin said. "I didn't expect you all to wait."

"Something I've been meaning to ask," Michelle said. "Did some member of your family starve to death, before I married in?"

"No. Why?"

"Because your mother seems terrified someone might possibly go hungry in her house," Michelle said with a smile. "We're about to have dessert. Triple-berry pie with ice cream. How on earth did you stay in shape growing up?"

Erin laughed. "I had three brothers. I had to be quick to get my fair share at the table."

"Anna!" Michelle called. "Come inside. It's getting dark."

"But mommy, I'm playing with Rolfie!" Anna protested.

"You can play with him in the living room," her mother said.

Inside, Erin got quick hugs from her brothers and her other sister-in-law Sarah, a firm handshake from her dad, and a big, warm hug from her mom. Then they all sat down at the table and dug into slices of Mary O'Reilly's homemade pie.

"Glad you could make it," Erin's dad said. "We missed you last year."

"You know how it is, working Patrol," Erin said. "They need everybody on duty on the Fourth, especially the single officers."

"That doesn't seem fair," Sarah said. "After all, you still have family, even if you're not married."

"Marriage is the fundamental building block of our society," Mary said.

Tommy, the youngest O'Reilly brother, and Erin's only unmarried sibling, snorted. "You know, marriage used to just be a convenient way of telling which man a woman belonged to."

"And now it's the other way round," Michelle said with a sweet smile.

"I think it works both ways," Sarah said. "In a relationship, each person belongs to the other."

"It's what binds us together," Mary said. "Erin, are you seeing anyone right now?"

"Not right now," Erin said, wishing this hadn't been brought up in front of everyone else.

"Whatever happened to that nice art dealer?" Mary asked, not taking the hint.

"I told you what happened," Erin said. "He couldn't deal with dating a cop."

"It can't be easy," Michelle added. "I worry about Sean whenever he's held up at the hospital, and his work's not nearly as dangerous as yours. I'd be a wreck if he was out there getting in gunfights all the time."

"By the time I see the results, the gunfights are already over," Sean Junior said. He was a trauma surgeon at Bellevue Hospital in Manhattan.

"Shelly, I was on the force twenty-five years, and I never

discharged my weapon in the line of duty," Erin's dad said. "It's a dangerous job, but there are lots of dangerous jobs. It's safer than being a fisherman, or a logger, or even a farmer."

"Maybe statistically," Erin's middle brother Michael said. "But the fish and the logs don't carry guns and knives."

"But what about the other man you were seeing?" Mary asked, pulling the conversation back toward relationships. "James, I think you said his name was?"

"It didn't work out," Erin said shortly. What she hadn't explained was that James Corcoran had turned out to be a mid-level member of the O'Malley Irish mob.

"So, how is it, being a detective?" Michelle asked Erin, recognizing the conversational dead-end and pulling a sharp U-turn. "Isn't it more interesting than patrol work?"

"Sometimes," Erin said. "But there's a lot of office time. And right now, we're stuck on our case."

"What're you working?" her dad asked.

Erin glanced at the young kids, choosing her words carefully. "You hear about that thing at the motel? Double vics, GSW?"

"That stands for gunshot wounds," Anna said with great seriousness. "I'm studying police terminal-ology."

"Terminology," Michelle corrected. "She's reading everything she can get her hands on about police work."

"Yeah, I read about the motel thing," Erin's dad said. "Sounds like a mob hit."

"I know," Erin agreed. "But it's not that simple."

"We can talk about it later," he said, catching Erin's meaningful look. "This is great pie, Mary."

It was. Erin's mom was an excellent cook, but baking was her particular specialty. Erin took a bite of pie, then got distracted by Anna, who was trying to sneak Rolf a mouthful under the table.

* * *

After dessert, the group fragmented. Tommy went out on the front porch to play his guitar. Mary sat on the porch swing, listening. Michael and Sean were talking baseball in the den. The Yankees had beaten the Twins 3-2 in Minnesota that afternoon, and Michael was doing well with his fantasy baseball league at work. Michelle was getting her children ready for bed, Sarah providing reinforcements. That left Erin and her dad. They went into Sean's office. It was filled with memorabilia of a career in law enforcement. Pictures of smiling, uniformed officers, newspaper clippings, various certificates of merit from Sean's commanding officers, and so on. There was also a gun cabinet, which was always kept locked.

"So, what's the roadblock?" Sean asked.

Erin sighed. "For starters, we can't ID the female victim. No prints on file, no identification. She was young, probably a Russian illegal, and had most likely been a prostitute. Maybe she still was, but we think she was trying to get out of the life."

"Human traffickers." His mustache twitched angrily. "Bastards."

Erin nodded. "Her pimp would be a suspect, if we knew who the pimp was."

"It'll be Russian mafia, I guess," Sean said. "You have contacts in that part of the underworld?"

"No," she said. "Vic Neshenko's poking around a little, but you know how it is. Nobody talks about the mob."

"Your last case was mob-related," Sean observed. "You cracked that one."

"Yeah, Dad. But that was the Irish."

"So? How'd you do it?"

"It was an internal thing," Erin said. "Competition in the

gang."

"You think that might be worth looking into?" Sean asked.

"How do you mean?" Erin asked. "Dad, I don't know who any of these guys are."

"Why not start with someone you do know? Lean on a low-level guy in the O'Malleys. Find one with a couple Vice busts in his jacket. He may know who the players are, and you'll have leverage on him. Use him to get to the competition."

"That's not a bad idea," Erin said. But even as she said it, she thought she might have a better one. A guy in the O'Malleys owed her a favor. But her dad had a history with the guy and wouldn't like that plan, so she didn't tell him.

*   *   *

The main event of the Fourth of July was the family picnic. Erin's dad grilled, while her mom filled the rest of the table with fantastic food. It felt like summer was supposed to feel to Erin. She remembered backyard grilling when she'd been a girl, and the smell of charcoal brought it all back to her.

Anna was playing at being a K-9 officer, calling commands to Rolf. The dog followed her patiently, but paid no attention to her orders. For one thing, she was speaking English, and Rolf had been trained in German. For another, while he was friendly to the girl, he had no respect whatsoever for her authority. Patrick trailed after the two of them, hesitantly patting Rolf's flank when he thought the dog wasn't looking.

"Just look at them," Michelle said. Her face was full of a love that made Erin a little embarrassed. It was so open and vulnerable, like the woman was watching her own heart running around outside her body. "Erin, haven't you ever wanted one?"

Now Erin really was uncomfortable. "Come on, Shelly, not

you too. Mom's bad enough. Every conversation I have with her these days, she's always asking about my biological clock. Like I'm a time bomb or something."

Michelle laughed. "That's not what I mean. It's just... I mean, how long have you wanted to be a cop?"

"Since before I was Anna's age," Erin said. "I think as soon as I understood what Dad did, I wanted to do it myself. I wanted it more than anything in the world."

"That's how I felt about children," Michelle said. "I know it's not politically correct these days. I'm supposed to have a career, to think of myself first. My mom's like that. She always wanted me to be, I don't know, a lawyer or a senator or something. But isn't the whole point of feminism that I can make my own choices?"

"I guess so," Erin said.

"And the first time I held Anna," Michelle went on quietly, "it was the best feeling I've ever had." They were standing a little apart from the rest of the family, but she still lowered her voice to almost a whisper. "You know, Sarah told me she and Michael have been trying to have a baby. She's got some kind of condition, though, and it hasn't worked so far. I don't know how she can stand it, poor girl. It would just break my heart. I'd have done anything, absolutely anything to have Anna and Patrick. I'm the luckiest woman in the world, I swear."

Michelle stopped talking. She looked at Erin, first with curiosity, then concern. "Erin? Are you okay?"

Erin blinked. "Yeah, I'm fine," she said. "Thanks, Shelly."

"For what?"

Erin was smiling now. "I get it."

"I'm glad," her sister-in-law said. "Look, Erin, you don't have to have kids if you're not ready for it. God knows there's enough unwanted babies out there already. And I don't mean to push you—"

"No," Erin said. "I mean, I get it. I know what Markov was doing with the Jane Doe."

"Erin," Michelle said, "I swear, you use real words, but sometimes I have no idea what you're talking about."

Chapter 9

Erin didn't wait to get back into Manhattan. She called Webb from the road a little after eleven that night. She'd stayed to watch the Woodstock fireworks with her family, then started driving.

"Webb," he said.

"I didn't wake you up, did I, sir?"

"Who is this? O'Reilly?" He did sound a little groggy.

"Yes, sir."

"Okay," he said. "For a minute there, you sounded a little like my first wife. I thought maybe I was having a nightmare. Or a child-support hearing. Which comes to about the same thing."

"Um... sorry." There didn't seem to be anything else to say on the subject.

"What is it, O'Reilly?"

"I'm on my way back. And I know what was going on at the motel."

"You got an ID for me?" Webb's voice perked up.

"No," she admitted. "But I know why Markov was meeting Jane Doe."

"She was a hooker," Webb said. "I thought we established

that."

"No," Erin said again. "Well, yeah, she was, I think. But that's not why he was seeing her."

Webb sighed. "All right, I'll bite. What were they doing?"

"Discussing adoption."

"Come again?"

"Natalie Markov said they really wanted a kid, but they hadn't been able to have one," Erin said. "The girl was pregnant. She'd kicked her drug habit, which suggests she was trying to have a healthy baby. Gregory Markov had a history of helping illegal immigrants."

"So, what... he was going to buy the baby?" Webb asked.

That took Erin aback. "I guess you could call it that. She'd have had trouble taking care of a kid, even if she was out of the life. I expect he was offering a better future for the baby. She was an illegal, after all. If she got deported, or arrested, or killed, at least she'd know her child would be safe."

Webb wasn't convinced. "Seems like a shaky motivation."

"With respect, sir, you're a man," Erin said. "Of course it sounds shaky to you."

"O'Reilly," Webb said. "Don't jump to conclusions. I've got two kids of my own, and if you think I wouldn't step in front of gunfire for them, you don't know what the hell you're talking about."

Erin swallowed. "Sorry, sir."

"Never mind. Does this help us catch the killer?"

"No. But I think it helps us ID the victim."

"How so?"

"We can check Markov's papers for payments to hospitals," she said. "She might've been admitted under an assumed name, but maybe not. And his files might have something on her. He absolutely had her medically checked out. Markov was a smart guy. This was a high-risk pregnancy."

"No kidding," Webb said dryly. "The mom's in the morgue. No, I know what you mean. And you're right. Run with it. Get hospital info to Jones and she'll help with the calls. You got anything else from your day off?"

"Not yet," she said. "There's a guy I can talk to, but I don't know if he knows anything."

"Okay, keep me posted. Drive safe."

"See you tomorrow, sir," Erin said and signed off. It was the Fourth of July, and there'd be more drunks than usual on the road. She needed to concentrate on her driving.

*   *   *

She made it home okay, despite a couple of close calls on the road. She thought about running down her other lead that night, but it was after one in the morning, she was tired, and she wanted to catch him alone if possible. Late morning was probably her best bet, so she went to bed.

By seven-thirty she was up and caffeinated, had taken her morning run and a quick shower, and headed in to the precinct. She was already appreciating the much shorter commute. It was even walkable in a pinch.

"Morning, Erin," Jones said from behind her computer monitor. "The LT said you've got something for me."

Erin explained her thinking. "I'll call Mrs. Markov," she finished. "She said she'd go through her husband's papers. I can tell her what we're looking for."

Jones nodded. "That'll help."

"Either of you two seen Neshenko?" Webb asked.

Erin looked at Jones, who shrugged. "No, sir," they said in unison.

It was almost eight-thirty when Vic trailed in. He had bags under his eyes and an enormous plastic cup filled with yellow liquid in his hand.

"Either it's time for your monthly piss test, or that's the most Mountain Dew I've ever seen in one place," Jones said. "You have a good time last night, Vic?"

Vic mumbled something inaudible and sat down at his desk hard enough that Rolf looked up to see what had happened.

"Take a good look, Erin," Jones said with a grin. "Vic Neshenko, departmental cautionary tale."

"You go down to Little Odessa last night?" Erin asked him.

Vic turned his head slowly, as if it hurt to move fast. "Yeah. What about it?"

"You find out anything?"

He tried to smile, but it didn't quite take. "Fantastic things. Unbelievable things."

"Right," she said. "Anything pertinent to our case?"

"Nope."

"You got laid, didn't you," Jones said. "I hope it was worth the hangover."

Vic took a long drag on his drinking straw and didn't answer. Jones quirked an eyebrow Erin's way.

"Take a look at that guy," she said. "I'll bet he doesn't even remember losing his virginity."

"Course I do," Vic said. He paused. "Just don't remember with who. Got a couple prime suspects, but not enough to charge 'em."

Erin shook her head and called Natalie Markov. The woman readily agreed to provide all the papers she could find. She even said she was headed into Manhattan for some legal arrangements a little later in the day and would drop the stuff off at the precinct.

"I don't think she killed him," Erin said when she got off the phone.

"If she did, she's the most helpful perp we've had in a while,"

Jones agreed. "Where you going?"

Erin had stood up and leashed Rolf. "To talk to a CI," she said. "See if I can get some info on human trafficking."

"Careful out there," Jones said. "I worked with some CIs on the gang task force. They can be a little twitchy. You want backup?"

"No thanks," Erin said. "I've got Rolf if things go sideways."

"I need to know where you're going," Webb said. "You want to go in alone, that's fine, but if you don't come out again, I gotta know what door to kick down."

"The Barley Corner," Erin said, and left before he could object.

*   *   *

The Corner was a classy Irish pub just down the street from Erin's new apartment. As she'd told Vic, it was the closest bar to her residence. It was also the closest Erin had ever come to getting blown to tiny pieces. The proprietor, Morton Carlyle, was a known upper-echelon member of the O'Malley branch of the Irish mob. He was a former IRA bombmaker and deeply involved with organized crime. Furthermore, he'd known her father from Sean's time on the force, and had given the elder O'Reilly some unwanted leverage that helped him survive a corruption investigation. He also owed Erin a personal favor. It was thanks to her and Rolf that his bar hadn't exploded in earlier that year. Carlyle was a lot of things, but he wasn't a man to forget a favor.

The breakfast crowd had thinned out by the time Erin and her dog arrived, which was just the way she wanted it. This wasn't a conversation that wanted an audience. She paused outside, squared her shoulders, and walked in.

The pub was nearly empty. Two guys were talking at a table

halfway down the wall, the bartender was polishing glasses behind the bar, and a waitress stood by the door. There was a man in the corner who caught Erin's attention. His haircut, a half-inch buzz, and the look in his eyes screamed military veteran. He calmly looked her over, and she guessed he'd ID'd her as a cop as easily as she'd pegged him. He nodded ever so slightly, then ignored her. She returned the favor. She'd seen him in here before and figured he was one of Carlyle's bodyguards.

Carlyle himself was at the bar in his place of honor, sitting on a leather barstool with his back to the bar, arms resting on it, watching one of the big-screen TVs. He was a slender man of about fifty, silver-haired, handsome and clean-shaven. He was dressed in a charcoal sport coat and matching tie and slacks, his shoes perfectly polished.

He smiled with genuine pleasure. "Erin O'Reilly!" he said, his accent pure Northern Ireland. "I've been hoping you would honor us with your presence." He stood up and offered his hand.

She approached and shook. His grip was firm. He held on to her hand just a little longer than the moment required. "Morning, Cars," she said, using his street nickname. "How's business?"

"Oh, grand," he said. "The lads do love their libations. On that subject, what can I provide for you? You've only to name it. On the house, of course. Your money's not accepted in any establishment of mine." He turned to the bartender. "Neil, give Miss O'Reilly whatever she might be wanting."

"It's a little early," Erin said, "but I'll take coffee. Cream, no sugar."

"You want a splash of Glen D in it?" Neil asked.

"No thanks," she said. "I'm working."

"And an Irish lass doesn't take her drink till the day's work is done," Carlyle said. "I'm sorry Danny isn't in yet. He works the evenings most days, but I'm sure he's wanting to thank you personally for saving him from a fiery death."

"Just doing my job," Erin said. "You and Corky helped."

"My pleasure," Carlyle said.

"What is Mr. Corcoran doing these days?" Erin asked.

"Since you've no information regarding that on your end of the business," Carlyle said, "I'm assuming he's getting away with things."

"Fair enough," Erin laughed.

"He does ask after you," Carlyle said. "He'll likely be in this evening, if you're wanting to speak with him."

"That's okay," Erin said. "I don't think talking is what would be on his mind."

It was Carlyle's turn to laugh. "You've the right of it, to be sure."

"Your coffee, ma'am," Neil said, sliding it across the bar.

Carlyle had a cup of his own at his elbow. He raised it, and Erin caught a whiff of whiskey from his cup. "Cheers," he said. "Now, what can I do to assist my very favorite detective?"

Erin had let herself forget how smooth Carlyle could be. She had to remind herself that he was one of the bad guys. "I'm working a case I was hoping you could help me with," she said. "I need some information."

Carlyle kept smiling, but Erin practically saw shutters clamp closed behind his eyes. "If you're asking me for knowledge of illegal activities, I don't see how I can help you, Miss O'Reilly."

"Relax, Carlyle," she said, trying to keep her tone casual. "This doesn't have anything to do with your people. I need to know about some Russians."

"Why don't you ask that oversized comrade of yours, Detective Neshenko?" Carlyle suggested. "He hails from that part of the world, if I'm not mistaken."

"I need to know about mob guys who might be involved in

human trafficking," Erin pressed on. "Russian Mafia types."

Carlyle wasn't smiling anymore. "Erin, these sound like dangerous men," he said quietly. "Men who wouldn't be wanting their doings discussed over coffee in a public house. I'd be very careful about such conversations, were I in your position. These men might not conform to your American ideas of how criminals ought to behave. Here, you've your own code of behavior, which even outlaws are bound to respect. That sort of men fail to make such distinctions."

"Look, Cars," Erin said, leaning forward and looking him straight in the eye. "These guys killed a man who was just trying to help someone out. And they killed a teenage girl. A pregnant girl."

"Really?" Carlyle sat forward, a look in his eyes Erin hadn't seen there before. "What information, exactly, are you seeking?"

"I have to find out who the girl was," Erin said. "And who she was working for." She took a deep breath and made the move she knew her dad wouldn't want her to. "I'd consider it a personal favor if you could ask some questions, find out what you can. After all, you owe me one."

Carlyle toyed with the handle of his coffee cup without taking his eyes from hers. "And you're prepared for the consequences, whatever they may be?" he asked.

"Always," Erin said, matching him stare for stare.

He nodded. "I know a few lads," he said. "I'll talk to them and see what I can discover. But I'll not be testifying, so that we're clear. And I'll speak only to you on this, not to any of your colleagues."

"This is between you and me," Erin agreed.

He smiled again. Erin put out her hand, but Carlyle shook his head. "No need for that, Erin," he said. "If we can't be taking one another at our word, then why are we even discussing this? Enjoy the coffee, darling. Come back tomorrow after supper. I should have something you'll be interested to hear."

"Thanks, Carlyle," Erin said. "I appreciate it."

"My pleasure," he said again.

Chapter 10

Natalie Markov had been as good as her word. Jones had three file boxes open at her desk when Erin got back, and she was up to her elbows in Gregory Markov's records. Vic was helping. He'd perked up a little and looked almost human again.

"How's it going?" Erin asked.

"If this detective thing doesn't work out, I think I might have a career with INS," Jones said.

"Don't even joke about that," Vic said. "Jesus. They oughta change the slogan on that statue in the harbor. Give us your poor, your weak, your huddled masses... so we can give 'em right back."

Erin hadn't ever worried too much about illegal immigrants. She'd always figured her time was better spent chasing real criminals, the ones who hurt other people. "Do we have a name yet?" she asked Jones.

"Not yet," the other woman replied. "But I think I'm closing in. I've got hospital records. Looks like there were a bunch of people who'd call him when they needed help with medical bills. That's where most of the five Gs went every month. He's noted down all the people he helped. It's in Russian, of course."

Vic nodded. "Shorthand, with shitty penmanship. This is worse than the birthday cards my grandma used to send me."

"We're making a list of names," Jones said. "We'll let the rest of you know. But there's more than one pregnant girl listed here." She looked up at Erin. "You really think he wanted this girl's kid?"

Erin shrugged. "Best theory I've got."

"I liked it better when he was a sleazy john and she was a no-good hooker," Vic said.

"Because it fits your cynical view of human nature?" Jones asked.

"Because I wouldn't feel as bad about them getting whacked," he said. "This guy's like Mother freaking Teresa."

Since she couldn't read Russian, Erin didn't have much to offer in the research department. She sat down at her own desk and scratched Rolf behind the ears.

"How about you?" Webb asked her.

"My guy's going to talk to one of his guys, then he'll call me tomorrow," Erin said.

"Which guy was it?" Webb asked. "Carlyle or Corcoran?"

Maybe it was residue from Carlyle's caginess, but Erin didn't want to talk about it in an open office. "He warned me about the Russian mob," she said, dodging. "He seemed to think they'd come after him, or even the cops, if they felt threatened."

"That's crazy," Jones said. "You get one nut job, sure he'll shoot it out, but even the real bangers know better than to take on the NYPD."

"I dunno," Vic said. "Russian Mafia, they're different. Where they come from, the cops are just the biggest, best-armed gang. You know how much corruption there is in Russian police departments? If these guys are overseas talent, we want to take 'em, we gotta be ready to go in with ESU."

"You sneaky little bitch, I got you!" Jones shouted. Everyone else turned to stare at her.

She gave an embarrassed laugh. "Ludmila Petrovna," she said, holding up a sheet of paper. "Bellevue Hospital, two weeks ago."

"Hey, my brother works there," Erin said.

"He an obstetrician?" Jones asked.

"Trauma surgeon."

"Then he didn't see her," Jones said. "This is our victim. I'm sure of it, but we can double-check blood type and some other medical indicators to confirm. It says she's nineteen, but that might be a lie. I've got blood pressure, pelvic exam, pap smear, the works. Looks like she was pretty healthy, in spite of the whole heroin thing."

"Lot of good it did her," Vic muttered.

"Is an address listed?" Webb asked. "How about emergency contact info?"

"There's an emergency phone number," Jones said. "It's... shit, it's Markov's cell."

"I was afraid of that," Webb sighed.

"But there's an address, too," Jones said. "Apartment, Brighton Beach."

Webb was on his feet. "I'll call Brooklyn," he said. "Get some uniforms there. And a CSU team. Let's move. Jones, you're with me."

"I'll ride with you and the mutt," Vic said to Erin.

* * *

"I moved to Manhattan so I wouldn't have to cross the East River every day," Erin said as they entered the Brooklyn-Battery Tunnel yet again.

"Funny how life works out," Vic said.

Ludmila's apartment wasn't far from the Markov residence,

but it was obviously a less upscale part of Little Odessa. The signs of storm damage were more apparent, as cleanup had been less of a priority, and the buildings were more run-down to begin with. There were guys on the corners that triggered Erin's Patrol instincts.

"See all the dealers?" she asked quietly.

Vic didn't answer.

"Vic?"

"Huh?" He blinked and looked at her. "What's up?"

"Never mind," she said. "You still a little hungover?"

"Maybe."

As they got to Ludmila's address, the dealers magically vanished. This was probably due to the two blue-and-whites parked out front and the pair of uniforms on the steps of the apartment building. It was a five-story brick walkup with several boarded-up windows. The detectives and parked outside.

"Everyone got vests?" Webb asked. "Good. Let's go. The apartment's number 419. There's two more uniforms up there already, so the place should be secure."

"Guess we should be grateful it's not all the way at the top," Jones said as they went inside.

Even though she knew there were cops already on scene, Erin had a hand on her Glock. She had a bad feeling. Part of it was Vic. She'd kicked in a few doors with him, and his focus had always impressed her. Now he seemed distracted.

"Vic!" she hissed.

"What?"

"What the hell is the matter with you? Get your game on!"

"Yeah," Jones said. "We run into a bunch of Russians with machine guns, I'm using you as a human shield."

"Thanks," he said.

"Knock it off," Webb said. He'd drawn his gun, a classic .38

Police Special.

Two more officers were waiting in the fourth floor hallway with the building super. He had his keys out and ready. The detectives stacked up outside the room. Erin got Rolf prepped, just in case. The shepherd was tense, ears forward.

Webb nodded to the super, who unlocked the door and stepped to the side. Webb rapped on the door with his knuckles. "NYPD! Open up!" he shouted.

There was no answer. Webb got out of the way. Erin looked at Vic. He'd pulled himself together. He returned her look, shouldered the door open, and went in fast, gun in hand.

It was a studio apartment, old and worn, but clean, well-kept, and empty. Clearing the space took only a few seconds. The tension drained out of the detectives, who holstered their weapons and started looking around.

"This isn't a hooker's place," Jones said. She was at the closet alcove, which had a curtain across it.

"How do you know?" Webb asked.

"The clothes," she said. "It's all conservative stuff. No bright colors, no fishnet stockings. The tallest heels are an inch and a half."

"You can tell a hooker by her wardrobe?" Webb asked.

"Can't you?" Jones shot back.

Webb thought it over. "Fair point."

Erin sidled over to Vic. "Okay, what's going on?" she asked in a low voice. "Seriously."

"Craziest coincidence," Vic said in an undertone. "I was here last night."

Erin didn't get it. "We didn't ID Ludmila until an hour ago."

"Not in this room," he said. "This building. Tatiana lives right down the hall. I had this crazy idea they'd turn out to be roommates or something when we got here."

"Holy shit," Erin said. "No wonder you freaked out. Which

apartment's she in?"

"423," Vic said. "Two doors down."

She shook her head in amazement. "You think they knew each other?"

"Yeah, that's a great idea," Vic said. "Girls love it when you ask them that. Hey, Anna, guess what? You were living down the hall from a pregnant hooker heroin addict, you know that? She just got murdered. And I thought, hey, maybe the two of you were friends. You wanna talk about it?"

"That's not what I meant," Erin said.

"Yeah, I know," Vic said. "And you're right, dammit. We need to ask the neighbors. I'll talk to her, next chance I get. But she's not home now."

"How do you know?"

"Because she had to go to work, okay?" Vic snapped.

"You were here last night," Erin said, finally getting it. "That's why you were late this morning."

"What are the two of you talking about?" Webb called across the room. "You taking a coffee break?"

"No, sir," Erin said.

"Then how about doing a little police work?"

They got back to business. Erin wondered whether she ought to mention Vic's whereabouts on the previous night, but decided against it. He hadn't known anything about Ludmila. It was just a crazy coincidence, like he'd said.

*   *   *

"So, what've we got?" Webb asked, later.

"She knew she was pregnant," Jones said. They'd found some prenatal pamphlets from the hospital.

"She wasn't turning tricks anymore," Vic said. There was no sign of her previous life. Ludmila's wardrobe, the lack of any sign of drug paraphernalia, no hint of the presence of a pimp, all of it pointed to a girl trying to get herself back on her feet.

"She was just a pregnant girl, sir," Erin said. That was the most heartbreaking thing about it.

"No, she wasn't," Webb said. "She had a past. That's the only hint of a motive we've got. And that's what's not here." He slapped the doorframe in frustration. "Washout."

They left the scene for the CSU guys, but without much hope they'd find anything. It was a demoralized crew that drove back to Manhattan, in silence most of the way. There didn't seem to be anything else to say.

Chapter 11

The following evening, Erin took Rolf home after work. She grabbed a sandwich from the deli half a block from her apartment, then went to the Barley Corner. She was still wearing her work clothes and her Glock. But she left Rolf behind. She didn't think she'd need backup. It was just a conversation.

The Corner was full of the dinner crowd, ninety percent male, eighty percent Irish, ninety-eight percent intoxicated. The Yankees game was on the big-screen TV, and the place was loud. Erin threaded her way to the bar.

A slim Irishman with flaming red hair, sparkling green eyes, and a truly devil-may-care smile appeared at her elbow like magic. "Erin, love!" he exclaimed. "I've been waiting and pining for this very moment."

"Evening, Corky," she said.

James Corcoran, handsome, charming, womanizer, scoundrel, happiest man in the Irish mob, beamed at her. "Where have you been, love? And why haven't you called? We had such a grand time on our last date."

"That wasn't a date, Corky," she said. "We were disarming a

bomb. That's business, not social. I hate to disappoint you, but it's business tonight, too."

"I'm wounded, Erin," he said, clapping a hand over his heart. "After all we've shared? At least give me a kiss, for old time's sake."

She smiled. "The times weren't that old." Despite knowing who and what he was, she couldn't help a little flutter of pleasure at seeing him again. "I think I need some more time to forget."

"If you say so, love," he said. "But time's running away from us, and we'll not be young forever."

"You gotta grow up before you can grow old," she said. "Anyway, I'm here to see Carlyle."

Corky cocked his head toward the end of the bar. "Usual place, love," he said. "I'll be here when you're done, nursing a drink and carrying a torch."

Shaking her head, Erin walked over to Carlyle. "Evening, Carlyle," she said.

"Evening, Erin," he said, nodding a greeting. "I see you escaped from Corky with your virtue intact."

"Barely," she said, taking the stool beside him that always seemed to be available. "You have something for me?"

"What are you drinking?"

"I don't drink on duty."

"And I don't work for coppers," Carlyle said. "So you can hardly be on duty, can you?"

"Fine," she said, signaling Danny. "White Russian."

"Fine choice," Carlyle said. "Glen D for me, Danny, there's a good lad."

He didn't say anything more until their drinks were on the bar. Then he picked up his whiskey and clinked the glass against hers. "Cheers, darling."

"Cheers," she said and took a sip. "So, you talked to your

guy?"

"I've made inquiries," he said. "And it's disquieting. These are some very unpleasant lads, Erin."

"Good," she said. "I'm looking for guys who did unpleasant things."

"There's a lad that's been mentioned more than once," he said. "He's Russian, and word is that he employs young immigrant women. He's the sort who takes unkindly to folk nosing into his business."

"What's his name?" Erin asked, leaning in closer. It was strange. They were having a sensitive conversation in a very busy pub, surrounded by dozens of people. The background noise gave them a surprising amount of privacy.

Carlyle took a slow, deliberate sip of whiskey. He leaned in close, putting his face just a couple of inches from hers. "Peter Vlasov," he said quietly.

"Where's he hang out?"

"There's a restaurant, Matrushka's, in Brighton Beach. Vlasov's family owns it."

"How do you know he's the guy we're looking for?"

Carlyle set his drink down. "I don't know anything of the sort," he said. "I'm no detective. You asked me to inquire about Russians engaged in unsavory enterprises involving young women."

"But there must be lots of guys in that line of business," Erin said. "There's thousands of hookers in New York. Why are you telling me about this one?"

"You're not looking for a pimp," Carlyle said. "You're looking for a killer, and he wasn't looking to set an example for his other girls."

"What do you mean?"

"A pimp will beat one of his girls, or cut her if she runs," he said. "He'll make it personal."

"Like a serial killer," she said.

"Just so," he said. "Why bullets? And why kill the man with her as well?"

"She was shot in the head," Erin said. "After she was already dying. They were trying to silence her."

Carlyle nodded. "Your killer treated her as a threat. And he was prepared to use automatic weapons to eliminate that threat. There aren't a great many lads in this town who'd do such a thing. Vlasov's one of them. I've not met the man in person, but from what I gather, he'll do absolutely anything to protect his interests."

"Okay," Erin said. "We'll check him out. But we need evidence."

"I can't swear to anything he's done," Carlyle said. "And I'll not testify in court. You'll have to find your evidence elsewhere. But if Vlasov was willing to kill twice on suspicion, he's the paranoid sort."

"That'll make it hard," she muttered, taking a sip of her drink.

"On the contrary," Carlyle said. He smiled. "Paranoid folk are predictable. They're easy to rattle. Make them think you're close on their trail and they'll panic."

"And they'll make mistakes," Erin said, returning the smile. "Thanks, Carlyle." She stood up.

"Your glass is still half-full," he said. "Sit down, Erin."

She hesitated. "I've got to get on this guy."

"He'll still be there," Carlyle said. "Drink with me."

Erin was impatient to be moving, but she sat down again and took another sip. "It's a shame to waste good alcohol. Thanks."

"My pleasure," he said. "And how's the family, then?"

She tried not to flinch. "My dad wouldn't want me discussing that with you. Hell, he wouldn't want me talking to you at all."

Carlyle chuckled. "You know, most would say I did him a favor."

"That's the problem," she said. "He doesn't believe in trading favors."

He hid his smile behind his whiskey glass. "Belief is a luxury. The world doesn't care what we believe, Erin. It just keeps turning."

"That's a funny thing for you to say," Erin said. "What'd you believe when you joined the IRA?"

He sighed. "I was scarce more than a lad. That was a great many years ago."

"What do you believe now?"

"I believe a man will do what he can, and what he can get away with. He'll take care of the ones he loves, and to hell with the rest. What did you believe when you put on the shield?"

"I believed I was making a difference," Erin said, meeting his eyes. "I believed my father was a good man, doing good work, and I wanted to do it too. I believed in catching the guys who thought they could do whatever they wanted, the ones who thought they'd get away with it. And you know what? I still believe it."

Carlyle was smiling again, but it was a softer smile than before, less amused. "God love you, Erin, you're still an idealist. I don't know how you hold onto it, but see that you do." His jaw tightened. "I know what you think of me, of what I am. But a man who'd murder a pregnant girl is a blight on this city. Take him down."

"I will," she promised. She drained the last of her drink. "Now I really do need to get moving."

"Of course you do," he said. He stood when she did. "Thank you for stopping by, Erin. You're always welcome here."

"You take it easy, Carlyle," she said. "Stay out of trouble."

"You too, Erin. Watch your step."

As she walked out of the Corner, Erin found herself wondering about one thing Carlyle had said. She didn't know how he could know what she thought of him, because she wasn't sure of that herself.

*　　*　　*

Erin called Vic as soon as she was out the door of the Corner. He picked up on the second ring.

"Neshenko."

"Hey, Vic? You still sober?"

"Sober as I ever am. What's up?"

"I got a lead on the Russians."

"Start talking."

She filled him in as she walked quickly to her apartment. "So, you want to go back down to Little Odessa?" she finished.

"Tonight?"

"Why wait? I want to rattle Vlasov, see what shakes loose."

"Just the two of us?"

"And Rolf."

"Okay. I'll meet you at the precinct in twenty. I'll call the Lieutenant, tell him what's going down."

Rolf had thought they were done for the night, so he was excited to be on another car ride. Erin buckled on her vest, fastened Rolf into his own armor, and pocketed an extra mag for her Glock, just in case.

Vic was waiting curbside at the precinct. He climbed into the passenger seat, a little awkwardly. He was wearing his vest, too, and it kept his bulky frame from bending easily.

"How good is your info?" he asked.

"I think it's solid," she said. "My guy's not totally sure Vlasov's our man, but he's definitely in the right line of business."

"We're rushing this a little," Vic said. He turned the keyboard of her car's computer toward himself and started typing. "We haven't done a full background on Vlasov. I called Jones. She's looking him up now, and she'll call us with whatever she comes up with." He paused, reading the screen. "Okay, we've got a whole bunch of priors here. A couple weapons charges, aggravated assault, pandering, compelling prostitution, sex trafficking... yeah, sounds like our guy all right."

"All that? Jesus. How long did we have this son of a bitch locked up?" she demanded.

"Most of it didn't stick," he said. "He did eighteen months on the assault charge, took probation for the weapon beefs. The rest of the charges were dropped. No witnesses. Looks like... shit, the sex trafficking charges were dismissed when they lost track of the girls."

"Lost track, as in they skipped town, or...?"

"They fished one of them out of the Lower Bay," Vic said. "Two others just vanished. Vlasov walked."

She gritted her teeth. "He threw them away."

"It's what happens when you treat people like things," he said with a shrug. "Once you cross that line, all sorts of possibilities open up."

They had a missed call from Jones when they exited the tunnel under the East River and got their cell reception back. Vic called her and put her on speaker.

"Peter Vlasov, born Pyotr," Jones said. "Age forty-five. Immigrated from Russia ten years back. His file's flagged by Interpol. He's got a few Russian prison tattoos, and he certainly did some time over there, but I can't get into the Russian files. I submitted a request, but knowing the way they work over there, we won't hear back for three to six."

"Days?" Erin asked hopefully.

"Months," Jones corrected.

"Assuming they get back to us at all," Vic said.

"We know about the stuff in his New York jacket," Erin said. "And we've got his mugshot. Anything else you can tell us?"

"Not much of a file on him," Jones said. "Otherwise we'd at least have deported him by now. I've got no associates, no operating area. Sorry, guys. All we have is a couple busts and a lot of circumstantial bullshit outside the assault rap."

"Okay," Vic said. "No big deal. We'll just act like we know more than we do. We drop Ludmila's name, that'll get his attention. I'll take the lead."

"Why you?" Erin asked. "I got the name."

"You think a guy like this listens to a woman?" Vic replied. "If we're trying to intimidate him, it makes more sense to have the big thug talking."

"Fair enough."

"The LT's in touch with Brooklyn," Jones said. "They'll have a couple blue-and-whites standing by, in case you need backup."

"He's not gonna start anything in his own restaurant," Erin said.

"You wanna bet your life on that?" Vic asked.

"I'm wearing the vest," she retorted. "We should be so lucky."

Chapter 12

Matrushka's restaurant didn't look like much from the outside. It was a refurbished brick building, heavy curtains blocking the windows. It was only quarter past seven, so the place was still open. Vic and Erin double-checked their weapons. Then they walked up to the door.

The interior was black, dark red, and dark-finished wood that made it look dimmer than the lights really were. The dining area was small, with high-backed booths that formed little alcoves. It was impossible to tell how many people were in the room.

"This is a tactical nightmare," Vic muttered.

A maître d' was in the entryway, a stout, balding man in a tux. He gave them a flat, unfriendly look, glaring at Rolf. "Good evening," he said in a thick Russian accent, but he didn't mean it. "Do you have a reservation?"

"Yeah, right here," Vic said and flashed his shield.

The man's eyes went flat and cold. He stood perfectly still, not saying a word.

"We're here to talk to Peter Vlasov," Vic said.

The maître d' pretended not to hear him.

Vic said it again, in Russian this time. He stepped forward, towering over the other guy. He added something else, also in Russian. Erin didn't understand, but it sounded pretty unfriendly. The man nodded stiffly, then turned and walked quickly through a door at the back of the room.

"What'd you say?" Erin whispered out of the side of her mouth.

"I told him it'd be in Vlasov's best interests if he talked to us," Vic said.

"That's not what it sounded like."

"I may have said it a little less polite than that," he admitted.

The wait felt long, but it was really just five minutes before the door opened again. A young blonde, barely more than a girl, came to meet them. She was wearing fishnet stockings, very high heels, a low-cut blouse, and a skirt that reached mid-thigh. "Please, follow me," she said. She laid a hand on Vic's forearm. He shook her loose and nodded to Erin.

They followed the girl through the door and down a back hallway into a private dining room, hung with red velvet and gold-braided rope. At the table sat a tall, gaunt man with dark hair and a hungry, wolfish look. Two big bruisers, so much alike that Erin was sure they were brothers, stood on either side of the man's chair. They were blond, blue-eyed, and muscular, their hands clasped in front of their belts. Their knuckles had tattoos all over them, and Erin bet if she got a look under their suit coats, they'd have more ink on their arms and chests.

"*Dobryy vecher,*" the man at the table said. "Or in English, if you rather. Good evening. Come, sit. Have a drink." He gestured to the table, where a vodka bottle and three glasses waited.

Vic remained standing, so Erin did, too. "Peter Vlasov?" he asked.

"Yes," the skinny guy said. "And your names?"

"Neshenko and O'Reilly, NYPD Major Crimes," Vic said.

"We need to ask you some questions."

Vlasov spread his hands on the tabletop. "Whatever I can do to help," he said. "But I doubt I can be of much service."

"We won't take too much of your time," Vic said. "We just need to know when you last saw Ludmila Petrovna."

"I do not know this name," Vlasov said, but Erin saw the flicker in his eyes.

So did Vic. "You know, that's a beginner's mistake," he said. "I thought you were more of a professional than that. Your experienced liar, he tells the truth till he's got no choice. See, now when I find out you do know Ludmila, and I know you do, then I'm wondering why you lied right off the bat. You've got something to hide."

"Your English is very good, Officer Neshenko," Vlasov said. "It is hard for me to understand all your words. But you are Russian, yes?"

"*Da*," Vic said dryly. "And so are you. But this is America, buddy. I know how you guys operate on the other side of the water, but this isn't your town. So, why'd you kill Ludmila?"

Erin was watching the hands of the big guys behind Vlasov. The one on the left unclasped his fingers and started moving one hand toward his jacket. She dropped a hand to her Glock and got ready to send Rolf into action, but the other big guy was already making a small gesture. The first guy reversed his motion, his hands still empty.

Vlasov's stare was flat and hard. "I told you, I do not know this person."

"Let me jog your memory," Vic said. "You and your guys took out her and Gregory Markov. Filled a Super 8 with MAC-10 bullets."

"Help me to understand," Vlasov said. "Are you arresting me?"

"Should I?"

"Since this is America, not Russia, I think I must call my lawyer," Vlasov said. "In this country, you have laws, so whatever you say, you must prove it in the courts. Otherwise, you are just exercising your jaws."

"I'll exercise my foot in your ass," Vic growled. "You listen to me, jerkoff. This is a courtesy call. We're giving you a chance to come clean. You give up the rest of the guys who did this, maybe you get out in ten to fifteen. You wanna be a hardass, that's on you. You go down for both of them, for the rest of your damn life."

Vlasov's eyes got even colder. "You are rude, Officer Neshenko. Uncultured. I would like you to leave now. I will remember you."

In answer, Vic forked his first two fingers at his own eyes, then pointed them at Vlasov and his two goons, one after the other. "We're done here," he said.

* * *

"That could have gone smoother," Erin said, once they were back in the car.

"You kidding?" Vic replied. "I thought it went great."

She raised an eyebrow at him and started the engine, not wanting to sit around liked a big target in a stationary car.

"He's our guy," Vic said. "When I dropped Ludmila's name, he practically had a heart attack. Right now he's sweating bullets. I wish we had enough for a wiretap. I bet there's some interesting conversations going on in there right now."

"How's that going to help us?" she asked.

"He's going to assume we're watching his whole network," Vic said. "A smart guy would go quiet for a while, just have everyone lie low. But not our boy."

"Why not?"

"Because he's a bully," Vic said. "A goddamn slave trader. Those two goons with him, he keeps them there because he's nothing without people to boss around. Guy like that, he has to show he's not afraid of us. Otherwise he loses respect. So he'll do something. We just need to keep our eyes open and move when he does."

"I don't like being reactive," Erin said. "Why didn't we slap the cuffs on him?"

"Tempting," Vic said. "But he'd be out in a couple hours, soon as his lawyer got downtown, and we'd waste more time on the paperwork than he would sitting in a cell. Nah, let him sweat where he is. I got ten bucks says he makes a move in the next twenty-four hours. The LT's got a couple units from Brooklyn staking out the place."

"No bet," Erin said.

*   *   *

Erin tried to get to sleep that night, but it wasn't easy. She kept replaying the confrontation with Vlasov, trying to think if she'd missed anything and to figure what would happen next. She should've frisked the bodyguards. She was sure they'd been armed, and there was no way they'd have valid licenses to carry. It wasn't much, but they could've pulled a couple of Vlasov's muscle guys onto the sidelines.

She turned over on her bed and sighed. Rolf shifted and sleepily nosed at her. She rubbed the base of his ears.

She didn't like it. Vlasov didn't give the usual signals of a criminal facing down a cop. Maybe Vic was right and he was just a bully, but she wasn't so sure. Carlyle had warned her about the Russians, more than once, and he was a man who didn't waste his words. In this, she trusted the Irish mobster's instincts more than her fellow detective's.

So what would Vlasov do? If they'd spooked him, he'd either make a run for it or he'd lash out. She wouldn't put it past him to have one of his guys take a shot at her or Vic. Vic had identified them by last name, but their addresses and phone numbers were unlisted, to prevent exactly this sort of thing. And Vlasov's gang's activities were confined to Little Odessa. It wasn't like they had their fingers in Manhattan. Then, O'Reilly wasn't the most uncommon name in the NYPD. He wasn't about to turn up on her doorstep.

If that was all true, why was she worried? She felt really jumpy, like a dog when a thunderstorm was on the way. She opened her nightstand drawer and verified that her Glock was within easy reach.

"Stupid," she muttered. A two-bit pimp wasn't about to declare war on the NYPD. She wondered what her dad would think of her, jumping at shadows and staring at the ceiling at midnight.

She put an arm around Rolf. She'd never admit it at the precinct, but it sure was nice having a partner she could cuddle. His furry body gave her the reassurance her own thoughts couldn't, and she gradually drifted off.

Chapter 13

They spent the next day building a file on Peter Vlasov. Jones worked her computer magic and found out that, in addition to Matrushka's Restaurant, Vlasov owned two nightclubs and probably ran an online escort service.

"Hard to tell for sure," she said. "But the IP address goes to the apartments over the restaurant, and I'll bet the whole place is full of his guys. I'm guessing some of the hookers live up there too, or at least do their business on site."

"Can we get a warrant, you think?" Webb asked.

Jones shook her head. "We can run it by Vice, see what they say, but this is way too thin. I mean, everybody knows online escorts are prostitution fronts, but they've got just enough legal cover that we can't move without proof of illegal activity. The best thing to do is probably to set up a sting, send in an undercover."

"I'll ask Vice for a guy," Webb said. "But that'll take time."

"I could do it," Vic said.

"Not a chance," Webb said, before Erin could open her mouth to say the same thing. "You've been face-to-face with Vlasov, and plenty of his guys may have seen you. You'd get made the instant you stepped inside."

"What about the nightclubs?" Erin asked.

"Nothing there, either," Jones said. "They're legitimate businesses. Probably fronts for the prostitution biz, but again, we can't prove it. The guy's slick."

Web sighed. "Sting it is," he said. "I'll call Sergeant Brown."

Brown agreed to put one of his undercover officers on the case, but warned it would take a couple of days to get him into action. They didn't want to rush it and risk the guy's safety. In the meantime, Jones worked Vlasov's financials, looking for a hit. Vic called the Russian consulate to see if he could get any movement on Vlasov's Russian police files. He was on the phone for an hour and a half, first in English, then Russian. Finally, he hung up, stared at his desk for thirty seconds without speaking, then clenched his fists and hammered them on the desktop.

"No good?" Erin said. She'd been scanning police reports for any sign of Ludmila Petrovna, hoping the girl might've been stopped by a Vice sweep, or maybe had some other minor infraction. Anything that could show a connection with Vlasov or any of his guys. Once they had a link, they could get their warrant. Then they might find weapons, get DNA samples, find the hard evidence that could close the case.

"They've assured me my request will receive special consideration," Vic said. "Don't hold your breath."

"Sure would be easier if we could do it like the old KGB," Jones said to him.

He snorted. "You mean, put Vlasov in the basement and pull out his fingernails? You think that'd work on a guy like him? These guys wouldn't talk to the Russian police, and they won't talk to us. You can't beat a confession out of Russian Mafia. That's fighting by their rules, and they're better at it than us."

"Besides which, it's against the law," Erin said. "And just wrong."

"O'Reilly's right," Webb said. "And the last thing we need is a soundbite like that, so can it. Even in the department. This is a clean office, and we're keeping it that way."

Jones grinned at Erin. "Guess that's the problem with being on the side of the angels, huh?"

* * *

The day slipped away in a haze of computer reports and research. A little after five, they packed it in. Nothing had happened.

Erin went by Vic's desk. "You want to grab a drink on the way home?" she asked.

"I could use one," he said. "This is giving me a headache."

"Count me in, too," Jones said.

The three of them, with Rolf in tow, went to a cop bar called Anonymous Tips just down the street from the precinct house. Erin got a Guinness, Vic had a screwdriver, and Jones went with a strawberry daiquiri.

"Daiquiri," Vic said. "You sure that isn't too manly for you? Maybe get a virgin Bloody Mary instead?"

"Okay, Vic I admit it," said Jones. "Your dick is bigger than mine. Slightly."

Erin had chosen the wrong moment to swallow, and almost choked on her beer.

The one drink turned into two, then three. All of them were glad to get out of the office and relax a little. Jones turned out to be a lot of fun off-duty, tossing one-liners back and forth with the others. Even Vic's sour mood was gradually improving. They ordered burgers and fries. The sun went down outside, and they hardly noticed.

In the middle of a funny story from Jones's gang squad days, Vic's phone rang. He looked at the screen, then held up a finger to Jones and answered.

"Hey there," he said, smiling. There was a pause, then the smile fell right off his face. "Are you okay? Where are you?"

Erin and Jones exchanged a worried glance. Erin put down her third beer, half-empty.

Vic was still talking into the phone. "Okay. No, you need to get somewhere safe. Look, I'm in Manhattan, but I can be there in less than an hour. Hey, no, don't... it's gonna be fine. I'm on my way."

He hung up and shoved the phone into his pocket. "I gotta go."

"What's the matter?" Erin asked.

"Anna's in some trouble," Vic said. "Forget about it." He started for the door.

"Wait a sec!" Erin said. "What kind of trouble?"

"Some guy spooked her at work," he said. "She got scared. Just needs someone to hold her hand. It's fine, Erin. I've got this."

"We'll get your tab," Erin said as he left. "You can get the next one."

"Who's Anna?" Jones asked.

"Girlfriend," Erin said.

"No wonder he's in a hurry," Jones said. "Y'know, it's always the big, tough guys who get wrapped 'round the girl's little finger."

"I hope she's okay," Erin said.

"Civilian problems," Jones said. "I'm sure she's fine."

Erin picked up her beer again with a shrug. "You're probably right."

"So, how about you, O'Reilly?" Jones asked. "Your love life in good shape?"

Erin laughed. "On life support. You don't even want to know about my last date."

"Disaster?"

"You could say that," Erin said, thinking about Corky Corcoran. "Nice enough guy, in his own way, but the whole thing kind of blew up in my face."

"Yeah, tell me about it," Jones said. "I haven't gotten laid in months."

They nursed the drinks and kept talking. Jones had a lot of interesting things to say about working the gang task force. To Erin's surprise, she was an advocate for legalizing drugs.

"Not in a free-for-all kind of way," Jones said. "Regulated, like tobacco. We can't get the drug dealers off the streets, they just get replaced by new ones. And we can't stop people taking drugs, because people are basically idiots. So we try to keep them safer. Get health screening, clean needle availability, take the supply away from the dealers and put it in legitimate hands. I'm telling you, it'd break the power of eighty percent of the street gangs in North America."

"And give us ten million new addicts to deal with," Erin said.

Jones shrugged. "At least the prisons won't be full of them."

"You can't change the law just because people aren't obeying it," Erin said.

"Why not? We did with Prohibition," Jones argued. "That's why we're sitting here drinking while our partner goes running off to save his damsel in distress, hopefully not picking up a DWI in the process."

"He was under the limit when he left," Erin said. "He's a big guy and he wasn't drinking fast."

"Say, have you met this Anna chick?" Jones asked.

"No," Erin said. "But Vic seems to like her. She's a Russian girl, interested in him. She pretty much fell into his life, he told me. What's not to like?"

"Hard to believe any girl would be that interested in him

right away," Jones said. "I mean, I'm not saying the guy wouldn't be attractive to the right girl, but the way he looks... God, your average girl doesn't go up to a guy like him and start chatting him up. Not if she's got self-preservation instincts. Erin, what's the matter?"

Erin's mind was racing. "Shit," she said. Everything had just fallen into place. She jumped out of her seat and fumbled for her phone. "Shit," she said again, punching Vic's number.

Jones put a hand on her shoulder. "Erin, what the hell is going on?"

Erin ignored her.

The phone beeped. Vic's voice came into her ear. "Vic Neshenko. Leave a message."

"Vic? This is Erin," she said. "Listen, don't go to the meeting. It's a trap. Call me the second you get this."

"A trap?" Jones was utterly confused.

"Come on," Erin snapped. She tossed a couple of bills onto the table to cover their tab and ran for the parking lot.

Jones followed. While Erin loaded Rolf into his compartment and got into her Charger, Jones hopped into the passenger seat, leaving her own car in its space. Erin peeled out, drawing an irritated honk from a taxi she cut off. Once she got on Broadway she turned on the siren and put the hammer down, flooring the accelerator.

"Jesus Christ, Erin," Jones said. "Will you just tell me what's happening?"

"We were waiting for Vlasov's move," Erin said. "This is it."

"Vic's girlfriend? What's she got to do with anything?"

Erin couldn't explain completely. She just knew it made sense to her. She gave it her best shot. "Russian girl, lives in the same building with Ludmila. Vic's in Little Odessa, asking questions about the shooting." A couple of cars and a panel truck were blocking their lane. She laid on the horn, siren still wailing. The truck slowly moved out of the way. She shot through the gap and kept hauling ass south. "This girl shows up out of nowhere, all interested in him. Now, right after Vic gets on Vlasov's case, she calls him and says she's in trouble, she needs him to come get her? No way it's coincidence."

"Why isn't he answering his phone?"

"He must be in the tunnel," she said. "No cell reception."

"I'll call Brighton Beach, get some uniforms," Jones said.

"And send them where? Vic didn't tell us where he was going!"

"Then what the hell are we going to do?"

Erin gripped the steering wheel, watching Lower Manhattan flash past them. "Try Vic's phone every couple minutes. We'll try to catch up to him on the way. At least we'll be close when the shit goes down."

* * *

The tunnel slowed them down a little, with a crush of traffic that couldn't, or wouldn't, get out of their way. They lost their own reception under the river. Erin squeezed the steering wheel hard enough to leave finger marks. Rolf, picking up on his partner's mood, wagged his tail and whined quietly.

The instant they cleared the tunnel on the Brooklyn side, Jones tried Vic again. "Nothing," she said. "I dunno. Maybe he's in a dead zone."

"Keep trying," Erin said. "No, wait. Call Dispatch, put Brooklyn on alert."

"Didn't I just say that?" Jones said.

"Sorry. Little distracted." Erin swerved around an oblivious minivan. She merged with 278 and kept screaming south.

Jones shook her head and got on the horn to Dispatch, giving them the short version. Judging from her reaction, she wasn't getting much help. Jones sighed and disconnected. "They'll do what they can," she said. "But Brighton Beach is pretty big. We've already got a unit by Ludmila's building. They're probably our best bet. They'll call if they see Vic. Does anyone know what this girl looks like?"

"Vic does," Erin said unhelpfully. She cut left onto the Ocean Parkway exit. A Camaro honked and crowded in on her, ignoring her flashers and siren. "How much paperwork would I need to fill out if I ran this asshole off the road?"

"Too much," Jones said. She was gripping the dashboard. "Do you really need to go this fast?"

Erin didn't bother to answer. "Try Vic again," she said instead.

Jones did. "It's ringing," she said. Then, a few seconds later, "It's still ringing. Does the stupid son of a bitch have it silenced?"

"Okay," Erin said, trying to think. "Call the precinct. Have them ping his phone and zero it in."

"On it," Jones said. "Should've thought of that."

It took a couple of minutes to get through, but the good news was that once she did, she didn't have to wait for a trace. That was Hollywood bullshit. With a live phone tied to Vic's name, and with GPS info built into the signal, they had his location instantly.

"He's at the corner of Brighton Beach Ave and Seventh," Jones announced. She checked their own position. "Take Ocean all the way to Brighton Beach, hang a left under the train tracks."

"Got it," Erin said. "Is he moving?"

"Don't know. He might be at a stoplight."

"How close are we?"

"A minute or so. Watch the turn. It'll be sharp."

Erin saw the train overpass ahead. She throttled down and swung into a hard left turn, tires screaming.

Jones had her phone to her ear again. "Vic? Vic!" she shouted. "Hey! Where are you?"

Startled, Erin fumbled the siren off so her passenger could hear. She left the flashers on and kept going.

"Vic, you've got to get out of there right now!" Jones snapped.

Vic's reply was so loud that Erin could hear it. "I'm fine! Anna, come on. We're leaving. What? Get down! NYPD!"

"Shit," Erin whispered. She heard gunshots.

Chapter 14

There were three distinct pistol shots, very close to Vic's phone. A man cried out. There was a crunch as the phone hit the ground. The connection went dead.

Erin reflexively punched her radio. "Dispatch! 10-13, shots fired, Brighton Beach Avenue and Seventh!" She rattled the words off as she tried to push the Charger's accelerator through the floor. They were only a couple of blocks from the corner. The nearest streetlights were out. She could see muzzle flashes in the dark under the train tracks.

"Erin!" Jones said, her voice pitched a little higher than usual.

"Not right now," Erin growled.

"Erin, I don't have my vest!"

Erin wasn't wearing hers, either. It was in the trunk of her car. She hadn't taken the time to get it out before they started driving. Rolf, of course, wasn't wearing his. They'd been relaxing after work, for Christ's sake, not gearing up for World War III.

No time to take care of it. She scanned the shadows, trying to figure out what was going on. There were at least three shooters and the muzzle flashes were big. Those weren't handguns. The men were using automatic rifles.

"Get the rifle," Erin snapped at Jones. She had an AR-15 in the car, though she'd always been better with her Glock. At least the bad guys were still shooting, which meant Vic was probably still alive.

Jones grabbed the rifle. Then they were on scene and there was no more time to think. Everything was action, training, and reflexes.

Erin slammed on the brakes, bringing the Charger squealing to a stop, angled half onto the sidewalk. She hadn't turned off the flashers, and the car was attracting all kinds of attention. Even as she unbuckled her seat belt and opened her door, she saw the flash of gunfire to her front. In a strange slow-motion daze, she saw a ragged line of bullet holes chew their way diagonally across her windshield. The first one was at the height of her eyes, but the recoil of the rapid fire pulled the follow-up shots higher, tracing an arc just over her head.

She had her door open. She slid sideways onto the asphalt, keeping the door panel between her and the shooter. Erin was uncomfortably aware that the door might stop a pistol round, but an assault rifle would punch right through. It was better than nothing, but not much. At least being behind the headlights would make it difficult for the bad guys to pick her and Jones out as targets.

Another gunman zeroed in on the car. A burst of bullets tore into the front grille. One of the headlights shattered and went dark.

Erin thrust her pistol just over the doorframe of the car and fired three quick shots at the nearest muzzle flashes. She had no idea if she'd hit anything. Jones had her own door open and was firing rapidly. Rolf, trapped in his compartment, was barking his head off.

Rolf. Erin reached behind her for the release on his

compartment. "Rolf, *fass!*" she shouted. There was no time for more detailed instructions. She just turned him loose and hoped for the best.

Rolf was out of the car so fast she hardly saw him move. He was a dark-pattern German Shepherd and was almost invisible in the shadows. The dog streaked forward, low and hard, toward the closest gunman. Erin let off four more shots over him. Somewhere to her left, someone else was firing a pistol, but she didn't know if it was an enemy, or Vic, or maybe even another officer. More bullets hit her car, punching holes in the bodywork. The window of her door shattered. A shot smashed the rear-view mirror just under her elbow. She didn't think she'd been hit, but couldn't honestly tell. The only thing she could think to do was to keep shooting, so she did. She shifted her aim away from Rolf's target, afraid of hitting him, and returned fire on the other rifleman.

The slide on her Glock locked back. She didn't remember firing seventeen shots, but the gun was empty. "Loading!" she called to Jones and dropped into a crouch, releasing the empty mag and reaching for her spare. As she slid it into the butt of the pistol, she heard more sirens, thank God. A man screamed from the direction Rolf had gone. Jones was screaming, too. Erin risked a sideways glance in time to see Jones toss down the rifle and draw her own Glock.

Erin came up with her gun reloaded, looking for a target. She didn't see any more muzzle flashes. Gradually, she realized they weren't taking fire. Jones had stopped screaming, but the man in front of them hadn't. That was the only sound besides the approaching sirens of an awful lot of police cars.

"You okay?" she called across the car.

"I'm fine," Jones said shakily. "You?"

"I'm good," Erin said, wondering if it was true. She didn't want to take her eyes away from the scene long enough to check for injuries, but she didn't feel any pain. She raised her voice. "Vic? You there?"

After what felt like a very long pause, she heard him. His voice came from the underside of the stairway on her left that led to the elevated train tracks. "I'm here."

"You hit?" she called.

"Fuck yes, I'm hit," he said. "Goddamn it."

Erin leaned into her car and grabbed the radio. "This is O'Reilly, four-six-four-oh. I need a bus at Brighton Beach and Seventh, forthwith!"

There was no answer.

"Dispatch!" she shouted into the handset again. Then she saw the bullet hole clean through the radio. She dropped the handset and went for her cell instead. It took a little longer. By the time she got an acknowledgment, the first backup cars were arriving on scene. Four uniformed officers jumped out of a pair of cars, guns drawn. More were coming. A 10-13 was guaranteed to bring every available officer at top speed. The 60th Precinct was only two miles' drive from the shootout, so plenty of cops had shown up.

Erin grabbed her shield in one hand and held it high as she ran forward, going for her dog. She found Rolf surrounded by cops. He was standing over a downed man, a skinny, dark-haired guy. An assault rifle with a banana-clip magazine lay nearby, spent brass scattered all around. He'd been taking cover behind a trash can on the corner, but Rolf's charge had flung him headlong onto the sidewalk. The dog had the man's arm in his teeth, jaws clamped tight. The little guy had stopped screaming, but that was probably because he'd gone into shock. Even in the limited light of the headlights and emergency flashers, he looked pretty pale.

Erin didn't care. "Take him in," she ordered the uniforms. Then, when they were ready with the cuffs, she called Rolf off.

He obediently let go of the man's arm and turned to her, tail wagging, ready to be praised. She envied her dog. This was all just a rough game to him. He was having a fantastic time. She, on the other hand, was starting to feel pretty shaky.

Erin caught movement out of the corner of her eye. Still jumpy, she swung around and half-raised her Glock. Vic was coming toward her, limping. He was leaning for support on a skinny girl half his size. The girl looked fine, but he had blood soaking the upper sleeve of his shirt and staining his left pant leg.

"Jesus, Vic," she said. "Sit down! You've been shot! Twice!"

"I'm fine."

Erin's emotions cut loose. "God damn it, you're not fine!" she shouted at him. "You're lucky you're still alive! Sit your ass the hell down!"

Vic blinked. To her surprise, he sat down on the curb without any further argument. "Just tell me one thing," he said. "What the hell are you doing here?"

"Tell you later."

"Got another one over here!" one of the uniforms called. A short distance away, partially screened by one of the train-track stanchions, lay another man. The cop kicked a rifle away from the downed man, but it was pretty obvious this guy wouldn't be doing any more shooting. He was lying in a pool of blood that was only getting bigger, and he wasn't moving.

"There's another by the stairs," Vic said.

"He dead?" Erin asked.

"I sure hope so."

"Oh, man," Jones said. She ran a hand through her hair, rubbed the back of her neck, and shook her head. "Oh, man," she said again.

Erin's phone rang. She was so hopped up on anger and residual adrenaline that she didn't recognize the sound right away. It rang two more times.

"You gonna get that?" Vic asked.

"Oh," she said, swiping the screen. "O'Reilly."

"O'Reilly, I'd like you to take a deep breath and think about your next words very carefully." Webb's voice was calm and quiet, which worried her a lot more than if he was shouting. "Then I want you to tell me just what happened. After that, you're going to go to the nearest precinct house and wait until I get there. Do you understand?"

She closed her eyes. "Yes, sir," she sighed.

*   *   *

Erin kept it together during her report to the Lieutenant. She stuck to the facts, ignoring the emotions that were right under the surface. Mostly what she felt was restless. She paced on the sidewalk while she talked. She wanted to hit something, to shout, to scream. She knew she was shorting Webb on the details, but she really didn't want to go into the whole thing right then. She finished her explanation, slipped her phone into her pocket, and took in her surroundings.

Jones was really shaken. She seemed disoriented and confused. One of the uniforms took her in tow, sat her down in a squad car, and gave her a cup of coffee. She'd gone quiet and pale. Erin thought the other woman might throw up any minute.

Vic tried to stay still, but like Erin, he was having trouble doing it. The girl at his side, Tatiana, was wrapped around his uninjured arm. She was crying softly and talking to him in Russian. Erin caught the name "Mila."

Rolf lay nearby, gnawing busily on his Kong ball. Erin had reflexively dropped his reward toy for him after getting him off the shooter, and that was all he was interested in at the moment. As far as Rolf was concerned, life was pretty good.

An ambulance pulled up, then more blue-and-whites and another ambulance. A couple of fast-responding news reporters were also on scene, but the Patrol officers kept them at a distance. The paramedics took charge of Vic and the guy Rolf had chewed on. Remarkably, no one else was injured. An EMT looked Erin over and found she'd gotten a small cut on her cheek, but she was otherwise untouched.

"Bullet?" Erin asked.

He shook his head. "Glass," he said, pointing to her car... what was left of it. Now that they had the illumination of a dozen pairs of headlights, plus the squad cars' spotlights, she could see the condition of the Charger. The windshield, front and back, were shot out. So was the driver's window. The body was peppered with bullet holes. The engine block had taken more rounds than she could count. The radiator was shot to pieces, the fuel lines torn up, and a mix of water, gas, and brake fluid had pooled under the car. Both front tires were flat and one headlight was out.

"Shit," Erin said, staring at her ride and trying to figure out how she and Jones had survived.

Another medic came over, leaving Vic in the care of his partner.

"How is he?" Erin asked.

"He's gonna be fine," the EMT replied. "Took one in the tricep, close-range handgun, right in the meat, through-and-through. Must hurt like a son of a bitch, but should heal up fine. The other one's a rifle round through the calf, also missed the bone. He was really lucky. It's all soft-tissue stuff, nothing to worry about."

"Good," Erin said. "I want him healthy when I kill him." She stalked over to the ambulance. Vic was sitting on the stretcher, gingerly rubbing his bandaged arm. Tatiana was still at his side, kneeling on the ambulance floor, holding on to him.

"Hey, Erin. Thanks for the assist," Vic said.

"Whatever," Erin said. "Is this Tatiana?"

The girl looked up at her, tears streaking her face. She nodded.

"You got a last name?" Erin asked.

The girl looked at Vic.

"Fedorova," he said.

"Tatiana Fedorova," Erin said, "you're under arrest for the attempted murder of a New York Police Detective. Turn around and put your hands behind you."

"Erin? What the hell?" Vic demanded.

Tatiana said something in Russian to Vic, clutching at him.

"You have the right to remain silent," Erin went on. "Anything you say can and will be used against you in a court of law, whatever language you say it in."

"She's a goddamn victim!" Vic snapped.

"That doesn't mean she's innocent, Vic," Erin said. She turned her attention back to Tatiana. She snapped one of her cuffs around the girl's right wrist, then twisted her around to face away. She did it briskly but not brutally. The other girl was smaller and weaker, and wasn't fighting back. She got the other cuff on. "You have the right to an attorney. If you cannot afford an attorney, one will be assigned to you by the court. Do you understand these rights?"

Tatiana didn't answer.

"Vic, does she speak English?" Erin asked.

He glared at her. "Look, just calm down a second."

"Will you use your head, for God's sake?" she shouted. "These guys were gonna kill you! How'd they find you? She's working with them, damn it!"

"They were shooting at both of us!" Vic shouted back. "They were gonna kill her, too!"

"What the hell difference does that make? These guys kill girls all the time!"

Vic started to say something else, then stopped. He turned to look at Tatiana, as if seeing her for the first time. "Anna," he said in English. "Why'd you ask me about the case? How'd you know Ludmila's name?"

The Russian girl stared at him. "Victor, please," she whispered. "I am sorry. So sorry."

"Vic," Erin said more gently. "We have to take her in."

He looked at her with eyes that had gone completely empty. "I know."

"Victor!" Tatiana begged. "They will send me back to Russia!"

"That'll be up to you," Vic said.

Tatiana straightened up. She blinked back her tears and stiffened her jaw. "I understand my rights," she said to Erin. "*Suka.*"

Erin didn't know the word, but from the tone of voice, she figured it was pretty accurate.

Chapter 15

They couldn't go straight to the 60th Precinct station, whatever Webb had said. Erin, Vic, and Jones had been participants in an officer-involved shooting. The patrol supervisor had already showed up. They had to turn over the guns they'd fired. That meant all three sidearms, plus the AR-15 from Erin's car. A Patrol Borough Shooting Team was getting thrown together. The District Attorney would get involved soon. Then there'd be a Grand Jury hearing.

In the meantime, of course, was the breathalyzer test. Erin remembered her three beers from earlier in the evening. The first two had been a couple hours ago, and the third wouldn't give more than faint fumes. She tried to remember how many drinks Vic had in him, but couldn't.

"I gotta say, I'm looking forward to the administrative leave," Jones said to Erin in an undertone.

"Why?" Erin asked. She hated being sidelined. Since it was their conduct that was being scrutinized, they weren't allowed to actually investigate the crime scene, and it was driving her crazy.

"No one shoots at you on admin leave."

"Hey, Kira?"

"Yeah?"

"You okay?"

Jones gave a shaky laugh. "I just got shot at with frigging assault rifles, Erin. Am I supposed to be okay after something like that? Are *you* okay?"

"They'll have the psych guys talk to us," Erin said. "They'll know better than me."

"We fired so many shots, I'm not even sure I can remember them for the firearms discharge report," Jones said, always mindful of the paperwork angle.

"You guys are fine," Vic said.

Both of them looked at him. It was the first words he'd spoken since Tatiana's arrest.

"They were already shooting when you showed up," he went on. "Your car looks like Swiss cheese. The Grand Jury's gonna think things over for half a minute, give you a medal, and let you go."

"What about you?" Jones asked.

He shrugged. "You said it, Erin. They were gonna kill me. I did what I had to do."

*   *   *

By the time they got to the 60th Precinct, all hell had truly broken loose. Reporters were all over the parking lot. The place was full of cops, jumpy as hell. Erin, Jones, and Rolf had hitched a ride in a couple of blue-and-whites while Vic went on to the hospital, and no one had ID'd them yet, but they were the only ones coming in with a prisoner, so attention zeroed in on them. They ducked through a volley of shouted questions like "Is this a terrorist attack?" and "Can you confirm that an NYPD officer fired first?"

They worked their way to the building, half a dozen uniforms clearing a path for them. Erin tried not to look directly at any of the TV cameras. She hoped Jones wasn't going to faint or puke. She kept a firm grip on Rolf's leash with one hand, and Tatiana's right upper arm with the other. Jones held the Russian girl's other arm and kept moving, staring straight ahead.

When they were finally secure in the station, Jones leaned against the wall and closed her eyes. Tatiana looked like she'd just gone through another gunfight. Her eyes were wide, staring right through them. Erin, still running on anger and adrenaline, went through the usual steps.

The desk officer looked them over. "What's the charge?" he asked.

"125.27," she replied. "Attempted first-degree murder of an officer. A-I felony."

The desk sergeant's eyes widened. "She's the one who shot up our guy?"

"She didn't pull the trigger, but she set him up," Erin said.

"She violent?"

Erin gave Tatiana a glance. The girl stared back defiantly. "Not yet."

"All right, she's high-risk, just on the basis of the charge," the sergeant said. He called two uniforms over for extra security. While they took charge of Tatiana, the sergeant grilled Jones and Erin about the arrest, including their use of force, Tatiana's condition, and what exactly had happened. The detectives knew they'd be telling the same story over and over again, but they tried to be patient while they talked it through.

Then, even though Erin had searched Tatiana at the scene, she did it again in front of the sergeant. This wasn't a strip search, but it was more thorough than the field frisk she'd already done. The girl didn't have any weapons. In fact, she was hardly carrying anything at all. She had a few dollars in loose bills, some coins, and a set of keys.

And then came the paperwork. Arrest report, voucher for Tatiana's keys, documentation checklist, and all the rest of it. While Jones started working on that, Erin turned her attention back to the prisoner.

"Miss Fedorova," she said. "You've got the right to make up to three phone calls, within the United States, no charge. You have anyone you want to call?"

"No," the girl said in a near-whisper. "I have no one."

"You sure about that?" Erin pressed. "Maybe call your pimp?"

"What for, *suka*?" Tatiana spat. "Maybe you think he offers you a job?"

Erin let it go. She'd had worse things said to her by plenty of suspects she'd hauled in. "So you're waiving your right to your phone calls," she said, just to be clear.

"Thrust your telephone up your ass," Tatiana retorted.

"Okay, y'know what?" Erin said. "I'd love to keep talking about this. It'd be fun."

"You would not know fun if it bit you on the behind."

"Dunno about you, Detective," the desk sergeant said. "But I'm pretty sure I would."

The two uniformed officers took Tatiana into the interrogation room while Jones and Erin kept working on the arrest report. Since Tatiana hadn't lawyered up, there was no real rush to talk to her, but the detectives knew they were under time pressure anyway. The Russians would be moving.

"We've got to get her talking," Erin said.

"I know," Jones said. She was still pale. She brushed back her hair with a hand that was trembling. "Seriously, Erin, I don't know if I'm up for this."

"Up for what?" Lieutenant Webb asked, walking up to the desk. He was scowling.

Erin spun around. "We've got Tatiana Fedorova in lockup," she said. "We've gotta take a run at her, get her to flip on Vlasov."

"In a minute, O'Reilly," Webb said. He took a long look at her, then at Jones. "You two okay?"

"Yeah, they missed," Erin said. "Vic got tagged, but he'll be fine."

"That wasn't what I meant," Webb said.

"Careful, Sir," Jones said with a weak laugh. "You're gonna make us think you care."

"Nah," Webb said. "You're a smart girl, you know better."

The door swung open again, hitting the wall with a bang. All of them whipped around to stare. Vic Neshenko stalked in. He was limping, disheveled, and sporting a pair of fresh bandages. There was a look in his eyes Erin didn't much like.

"Where is she?" he demanded.

"Interrogation room," Erin said. "What are you doing here?"

"We gonna throw that question at each other all night?" Vic shot back. "I don't need a hospital. I got 'em to turn the ambulance around."

"Vic, you've been shot," Jones said. "Twice."

He shrugged. "I'll live. We need a warrant to get Vlasov, and the rest of his goons if we can. The guy Rolf bit is going into surgery, so he won't be talking for a couple hours. The medics said the dog broke a couple bones in his arm."

"Good boy," Erin said, rubbing Rolf behind the ears.

"So we haven't got a choice," Vic finished. "I'm going in." He started for the interrogation room.

"No!" Erin exclaimed.

Everyone stopped. Webb raised an eyebrow. "You giving orders, O'Reilly?" he asked quietly.

"Sir, he can't go in there!"

"Of course I can," Vic said.

"No, he can't," she said. "She's his girlfriend!"

"That's why she'll talk to me," he said.

"That's why he can't talk to her," she persisted, still talking to Webb. Her voice was rising, but she didn't care. "Let me do it. He's too emotionally involved!"

"And you're not?" Webb snapped back.

"Like hell I am!"

"Listen to yourself!" the Lieutenant fired back. "Get your monkey-brain out of the driver's seat and try to think like a cop, for God's sake! Forget how you're feeling and think about what we need from the girl. How are we going to get it?"

"Monkey-brain?" Erin echoed. Her fists were clenched. She was awfully close to saying or doing something that might get her thrown off the force.

Webb's face softened a little. "Erin, you're a better cop than this," he said. "You're a better detective than this."

"She tried to warn me," Vic said softly.

"Huh?" Erin looked at him.

"She was at the bar on the corner," he said. "I couldn't park right in front. I got out of the car and she came out the door. There was this guy there. Just as he was walking toward me, she looked at me, flipped her eyes at him, and told me to run."

"She still set you up," Erin said.

"I need to know why," he said. "I need to, Erin. And she'll tell me. She won't tell you, or anyone else."

"She's a hardened street kid," Jones said. "I met a bunch of them on the gang task force. You threaten them, they just turtle up."

"She did what she had to," Vic said. "But she didn't want me to get killed. I can use that."

Webb nodded. "Go on in," he said. "The rest of us will observe."

"We need another cop in the room," Erin said.

The Lieutenant shook his head. "This has to be one-on-one," he said. "It won't work otherwise."

Vic limped to the door. He turned with his hand on the knob. "It's okay, Erin," he said with a hint of a smile. "You can have the next one."

"Hey, Vic?" she asked.

"Yeah?"

"What's *suka* mean?"

Then he did smile, just for a moment. "It's Russian for 'bitch.'"

"Damn right I am," Erin said.

* * *

Webb, Jones, and Erin watched the interrogation room through the one-way mirror. A Russian-American cop from the 60th was there, by Webb's request, in case any Russian got spoken. Tatiana sat cuffed to the table in the room, staring at the stainless-steel surface in front of her. The girl's jaw was so tight Erin could see the muscles of her face trembling.

"What do you think?" Webb murmured.

"She's a tough one," Jones said.

"But she's brittle," Erin added. She was still pissed off, at Tatiana, at Vic, at Vlasov, at Webb, at pretty much the whole world. She'd calmed down just enough to recognize Webb had probably been right to keep her out of that room. Angry cops interrogating suspects led to nothing but trouble, and sometimes lawsuits. But that didn't mean she had to be grateful to him.

"You're right," Webb said. "If all we were after was a confession, we could break her down. But we need her on our side. You think Neshenko's up to the job?"

"Find out in a minute," Erin said without looking at him.

The door to the interrogation room opened and Vic limped in. Tatiana took a deep breath and looked up. When she saw who it was, her eyes widened.

"Victor?"

"She's confused," Webb said, mostly to himself. "Throws her off balance. Good."

"Hey, Anna," Vic said. He crossed the room and took a cuff key out of his pocket. "Let's get these off you."

"You are not afraid of me?" she asked, her mouth twisting into a wry half-smile.

He unfastened the cuffs. "Course not," he said. "You don't want to hurt me."

"Your friends think I do."

Vic snorted. "You wanted me dead, I'd be dead now." He sat down in the chair opposite her. "It's okay, Anna."

"You are not angry with me?" she whispered.

He shook his head. Then he reached across the table and laid his hand over hers. Erin knew this was risky. Any physical contact in an interrogation room could be twisted by a lawyer to look like coercion. Cops were allowed to lie and cheat, but they were absolutely not allowed to beat confessions out of suspects.

Tatiana swallowed. A tear spilled out of her eye and rolled down her cheek.

"Anna, you already helped me tonight," Vic said. "You warned me about the gunman. I need you to help me some more, and to help yourself."

"I am cop-killer," she said bitterly. "That is what they call me. How can you help me?"

"They made you do it, didn't they?" Vic said, keeping his voice quiet and reassuring.

She hesitated, then nodded. "There was a man at the telephone with me."

"Was it one of the guys who was waiting for me?"

"Yes."

"Which one?"

"The one with the pistol. The one you shot."

"What was his name?"

Tatiana hesitated again.

"Anna, he's dead," Vic said. "It doesn't matter to him."

"Alexei."

"Do you know Alexei's last name?"

"Borodin."

"On it," Jones said. She'd borrowed a laptop from the boys in the 60th. It was already open and powered up. She started typing.

"Anna," Vic said. "Can you tell me what happened? From the beginning?"

She lowered her head so her hair fell in front of her face. Then she nodded. Still looking down, she started talking.

"I was born in little village north of Saint Petersburg. Volochaevka. You do not know it. When I am sixteen, I meet a man from the city. He seems nice man, good clothes, talks well, expensive shoes. He tells me there is job in Saint Petersburg for pretty girl, as waitress. Maybe singer in club. He gives me telephone number. I am stupid. I go to city on weekend, make telephone call, go to club. They give me drink. I go to sleep.

"I wake up in metal box. Box moves up and down, side to side. There are other girls with me, no lights. We talk quietly. If we are not quiet, men hit sides of box, shout at us. They give us little food, water. We decide we are on ship.

"I do not know how many days we are on ship. Sometimes men come, they take one, two of the girls. They bring them back, the girls are hurt, bleeding, crying. Then... they take me."

Vic didn't want to ask, Erin could see it in his eyes, but he was a good cop in spite of it, and he had to ask the question, had to establish the crimes that had occurred. "Did they rape you?"

"Yes." Tatiana tried to pull her hands away from him. Vic held on with one hand. With the other he wiped away one of her tears. She wasn't able to go on for a few minutes. He let her take her time. The detectives watched her pull herself together, rebuild some of her psychic armor.

"I do not see statue when we come to New York," she finally went on.

"Statue?" Vic echoed.

"Big green statue," Tatiana said. "Lady Liberty. I am still in box, no windows. I would like to see her. I have never seen her."

"She's in the harbor, right there," Vic said. "You can see her from Manhattan."

"I never leave Little Odessa," she explained. "They do not let me go."

Vic wanted to say something else, but didn't. He kept holding her gently, but his eyes showed nothing but pure, murderous rage.

"They put me in apartment with bars on the windows," she continued. "There are other girls there, many girls. They do not let us out during the day, not at first. Later, only with one of them. They bring the men to us, to our rooms. They give to us pills, and needles. With the needles, it is not so bad. The needles make us not to care so much. We dream without sleeping, and we feel nothing.

"I am there three, four months, I think. I become a little friends with some of the other girls. One of them, Ludmila, has still a little hope. She knows a name, she has heard it. It is name of a man, a good man who helps people like us."

"What's the name?" Vic asked. They already knew the answer, but he needed it for the record.

"Gregory Markov," Tatiana said. "Ludmila, she makes plan. I help her. Sometimes man comes, wants two girls at same time. We work together. While I keep his attention, she takes phone from his jacket, hides it under mattress. When he goes, she calls information number, gets number of Gregory Markov."

"Why not call the police?" Vic asked.

She gave him a look that told the whole history of the NYPD, the Russian police, and police corruption in general. "And tell them what? We are criminals. They will lock us away, or send us back to Russia. I cannot go home. I am ruined, broken. My papa, he will not let me come back. All that is waiting in Russia is same thing.

"But Mila has hope, and she has Gregory's name. She calls him on cell phone, very careful, very quiet. We do not know where we are, but she tells him name of man who owns apartment. He says he will use name, will come to find us and help us."

"Anna," Vic said. "What's his name?"

"He will kill me," Tatiana said.

"No," Vic said, "he won't."

"You will protect me?" She took hold of his fingers in both hands.

"I promise," he said. "But for me to be able to do that, you have to tell me what you know."

"His name is Pyotr. Pyotr Vlasov."

"That's it," Webb said triumphantly. "That's our warrant." He snatched out his phone and speed-dialed a judge.

"Good," Vic said. "We can get him now, arrest him. He'll never be able to hurt you, or another girl, again."

She shuddered. "Six, seven days go by. Mila is afraid. She takes apart cell phone, flushes it down toilet, so they do not find it. We cannot talk to Gregory. I am not hoping, but she says he will come. She says he has kind voice." She looked at Vic. "Like you."

"First time I've heard that about Vic," Jones muttered.

"Then he comes," Tatiana went on. "He pretends he is just

another man. But Mila tells me what he does. He does not touch her. He gives to her some money, new phone to hide. He tells her where to go, what to do. Then we wait.

"The men with us, they are sometimes careless. They drink vodka, get drunk and sleepy. One night, Mila sees chance. She runs away. She tells me to go with her. I am afraid, but I tell myself I must be brave. We run, together.

"We are lost. We know no one. But we have Gregory and his telephone. Mila calls him. He comes to get us, takes us to apartment. He pays rent for us, brings us clothes. He tells us we are safe.

"It is not easy. We start to miss the needles, the pills. We are sick. I think Mila will die, she is so sick. I want to die. I try. I cut my arms with kitchen knife to make pain stop." She turned her arms over and showed a pair of ugly crosswise scars on her wrists. "But I have no strength. I cannot cut deeply. I bleed little while, then stop. I get better. But Mila is still sick. After little while, we find out she will have baby.

"Mila does not want to be mother. She knows she cannot take care of baby. She talks to Gregory, asks him what to do. He takes her to doctor, helps her. He finds job for her, for me.

"Gregory tells Mila not to kill baby. He says he and his wife have no baby, that they always want baby, but something is wrong and they cannot. He says baby is gift from God, not to throw away. Mila tells me, she has idea. She will give baby to Gregory and his wife. They will be happy, and baby will have happy life.

"We go on three, four months more, no problem. I move into my own apartment, down the hall from Mila. Is more space for her, for when baby comes. Then one day, I am working, as waitress in coffee-house, and Yuri comes in."

"Who's Yuri?" Vic asked.

"Yuri is man who works for Pyotr," Tatiana said. "Is little

man, eyes like rat, little mustache."

"Sounds like the guy Rolf chewed on," Erin commented.

"Hope he doesn't get indigestion," Jones said.

Webb hung up from his phone call. "We'll have the warrant as soon as the judge gets it to us," he said. "We can grab Vlasov, plus any of his known associates. What'd I miss?"

"They got out," Erin said. "Markov set them up with a place to stay."

"Shush," Jones said. "They're talking. Get it from the recording later."

"I hide in kitchen when I see him," Tatiana said. "I think maybe he misses me. I tell manager I am sick, go out the back door, run to apartment.

"When Mila comes home from work, I tell her. She calls Gregory, tells him she is afraid, but that she has something important to tell him. She will meet him somewhere else, at motel. She tells me where.

"Mila goes to motel to meet Gregory. She will tell him her idea for baby, ask him to take both of us out of city right away. I wait at apartment."

Tatiana stopped. She pulled her hands back from Vic again, and this time she managed to disentangle herself. She buried her face in her hands, shoulders shaking.

"If I go with them, maybe nothing happens," she said through her sobs. "But I stay. I am tired, and afraid to move. I think if I hide, maybe everything is okay. I think if I go outside, maybe Yuri sees me.

"He followed me. Yuri and Paul come to my apartment."

"Paul?" Vic prompted.

"Paul Ivanov. He has brother, Dmitri. Both of them work for Pyotr. Dmitri was soldier, in Spetznaz. How do you say?"

"Special Forces," Vic said.

"Yes," Tatiana agreed. "Paul is not soldier. He is in prison in

Russia, then comes to America. He is big, strong. Yellow hair, blue eyes, lots of drawings on arms."

"Yeah, I've met him and his brother," Vic said.

"Paul knows how to open locks. They come in while I am in shower, drag me out. Paul has knife. He tells me he will cut my eyes, make me blind. He will... he will cut me... in other places. Yuri will help him. Yuri likes to hurt girls. It makes him excited."

Erin was getting less and less sorry about Rolf biting the son of a bitch.

"They want to know where Mila has gone," Tatiana said miserably. "I do not want to tell them. Yuri takes cigarette lighter, burns bottoms of my feet. Paul is ready to cut me. I am sorry, Mila. I am so sorry!" Her voice ended in a wail.

"You told them where she and Gregory were," Vic said. "It wasn't your fault, Anna. They made you do it."

"Paul takes telephone, calls Pyotr," Tatiana said dully. "He leaves, Yuri stays with me. Yuri... hurts me. After couple hours, Paul comes back. Dmitri is with him. They tell me Mila is... is dead. They take me back to apartment with other girls.

"Then you come to Little Odessa, asking questions about Mila." She looked back at him. "Pyotr talks to me, tells me he needs to know what you know. He tells me to talk to you, be your friend. I am to be spy. If I do not do it, he says he will kill me, you, and all the other girls."

"Did he tell you to screw me?" Vic asked, and his voice had a sharp edge to it.

She flinched, but didn't look away. "No. That is because I want to."

Webb glanced at Erin, eyebrows raised. "You knew they were sleeping together?"

Erin nodded, then tilted her head back toward the interrogation room, not wanting to interrupt.

"I talk to you," Tatiana said. "I think you are good man. You are strong man, maybe protect me. I think... maybe I can trust you."

"Why didn't you tell me then?" Vic asked. "You didn't have to go back to them."

"I am afraid," she whispered. "All the time, I am afraid. You do not know. I am weak, maybe. I am sorry."

It was Vic's turn to flinch. "No, I'm sorry, Anna," he said. "I can be an asshole sometimes. It's not your fault. It's those bastards who did this to you."

"I tell Pyotr you do not know anything," she said. "I try to protect you. But then you come to Pyotr's restaurant, with other cop, the *suka*. Now Pyotr is afraid. He knows you know it was him who killed Mila and Gregory.

"So Pyotr has plan. He has me call you, tell you I am in trouble. He tells me where to meet you. His men are there. Alexei will shoot you, take wallet, make it like robbery.

"I tell myself to be brave. Alexei is with me until he sends me out to wait for you. Then I tell you to run."

"I wasn't going to leave you there," Vic said.

She gave him a weak smile. "You are faster and stronger than I thought," she said. "Alexei already has gun in hand, but you are too fast for him."

"He was quick, too," Vic said, rubbing his wounded shoulder.

"The rest you know," she said. "You shoot Alexei. There are others waiting, with rifles. You grab me, throw me down. Then other police come, shoot at Pyotr's men. Now we are here."

Vic nodded. "Yeah. And you're safe. Listen, Anna, you're gonna have to stay here, in the police station. They'll lock you up, but that's to keep you safe, okay?"

"You stay with me?"

"I can't," Vic said, standing up.

"Why not?" Tatiana asked, fear shooting into her face again.

Vic's eyes were hard as blue ice. "We're going after Pyotr and his asshole friends," he said. "And we're taking them the hell down."

Chapter 16

Vic stalked out of the interrogation room. The other detectives met him in the hallway outside. Erin stepped toward him. There were a lot of things she wanted to say.

"Vic—" she began.

"Not now," he cut her off. Then, to Webb, "You got the warrants?"

"Yeah," Webb said. "We're gonna call in ESU to deal with this."

"Good idea," Vic said. "I know some of the guys from the Brooklyn team. We can ride along with them."

"Hold on, Neshenko," Webb said. "They're going in to serve the warrants. We're going to wait outside."

"The hell we are."

"No way!" Erin said simultaneously.

Webb sighed. "Vic, you got shot earlier this evening. You've killed one man, maybe two. Erin, Kira, you've been in a gunfight. One of you probably took out that other gunman. Technically, you were on modified assignment as of the moment the Patrol Commander took over the shooting site. You're not even supposed to be carrying weapons until the incident's closed."

"Bullshit," Vic snapped. "This is our case. We've gotta see it through."

"You're not going in there," Webb said.

"Stop me."

The two men were eyeball to eyeball. Vic was three inches taller than Webb and outweighed him by at least twenty pounds in spite of the Lieutenant's middle-age spread. But the older man didn't back down. His face was just as hard and firm as Vic's.

"Look," Webb said. "Vlasov's goons have military training, some of them. They've got army-issue weapons. These are dangerous guys. ESU's going to knock down their doors. If you go in there, already wounded, you're going to put the rest of the team in danger. I know you don't want to do that. This isn't about finishing what you started, or being tough enough. I know damn well you're plenty tough. But sometimes the other guy's got to go through the door first. We'll ride along to the scene and observe. But that's all we can do."

For a second, Erin thought Vic was going to slug his commanding officer. Instead, he slammed his fist into the wall. There was a muffled crunch, and when he pulled his hand back there was plaster dust on it and a dent in the wall.

"You know what they did to her," he said through gritted teeth.

Webb nodded. "We'll get them," he promised.

*　　*　　*

The ESU tactical team assembled at the 60th Precinct parking lot. The tactical guys geared up with full body armor and helmets, bulletproof shields, breaching shotguns, submachine-guns, and assault rifles. Sniper teams, battering rams, a bomb-squad guy with a remote-control robot, the whole works. When everyone was prepped, they saddled up and drove to a staging point, a parking garage two blocks east of Matrushka's. Erin rode along with Vic, Rolf in the back seat. Jones and Webb rode in the ESU's command van.

"You want to talk about it?" Erin asked.

"Not really," Vic said.

"Still pissed at me?"

"Not really," he said again.

"I think they'll let Tatiana go," Erin said.

Vic grunted.

"Maybe we can figure a way to get her a green card," she said. "There might be some strings we can pull."

"Later, Erin," Vic said. "We got a job to do."

They parked next to the command van. Even though they wouldn't be going in, the detectives wore their vests. Getting caught without them once was plenty. Webb and the ESU commander, a gray-haired lieutenant named Sanders, were scanning blueprints of the restaurant.

They had two nightclubs to hit in addition to Matrushka's. That meant three strike teams, plus backup units to surround the buildings and provide cover. This was a major tactical operation, laid down on very short notice, and Erin could feel the tension in the van. But these guys were professionals. They made their plans quickly and calmly.

It took a while to get everyone in position. The detectives watched on monitors in the van, leaning over the communications guy's shoulders. It was almost three in the morning when all the pieces were set. There were squad cars setting roadblocks on either end of all three blocks, snipers on opposite rooftops, and breaching teams standing ready. Erin realized she was holding her breath and told herself to breathe normally.

"All units, execute," Sanders said.

The tactical teams exploded into action. They rammed the doors open and poured into all three buildings in unison. They hurled flashbangs around corners. Bright, white light burst on the monitors as the nonlethal grenades detonated. The radio waves were full of officers shouting. People in the nightclubs were screaming.

But there was no gunfire. Erin felt relieved at first. Then, as the seconds passed, she started to wonder. Everything was going too smoothly. The assault teams had secured the main rooms of the nightclubs and the dining area of the restaurant, but there was no sign of Vlasov or his guys.

She glanced at Vic and saw the same look in his face. She felt a sinking feeling in her gut.

"They're already gone," she said.

Vic nodded. "They must've booked it as soon as the ambush went sideways. Christ, they've had hours to get out."

Webb grabbed the van's radio. He put out a BOLO on Vlasov. Inside half an hour there'd be a massive, citywide manhunt underway. The NYPD didn't screw around when one of their own got bushwhacked. But it was all going to be too late.

"What can we do?" Jones asked.

Erin had one idea. It was slim, but it was the best shot she had. She stepped out of the van and brought up her smartphone. She looked up a number and dialed it.

"Barley Corner," said a perky young woman with a charming Irish brogue. "This is Caitlin. What can I do for you?"

"I need to talk to Mr. Carlyle," Erin said. "Right away."

"What is your name, ma'am?"

"Erin O'Reilly. Tell him it's important."

"Just a moment, ma'am," Caitlin said, putting her on hold. Erin kept walking, putting some distance between her and the ESU van. She didn't want Carlyle's name getting dragged into this if she could help it.

More time passed. It wasn't very long, less than a minute, but it seemed longer.

"Erin!" Carlyle said. "I'm delighted to hear your voice. I've been a mite worried about you, darling."

"I'm in a hurry, Cars," she said. "I need to know more about the Russians."

His voice sharpened. "I told you these were dangerous lads. I saw what happened on the telly. Are you wounded?"

"No, but some other guys are," she said. "Listen, they're making a run for it. I need to know where they're going."

"Russia, of course. You hardly need me to tell you that."

She closed her eyes and willed herself to be patient. "Yes, I know that. But how are they getting out of New York?"

"Private charter flight," he said, no hesitation.

"You sure?"

"It's what I'd do, were I in a delicate situation with law enforcement. They've likely got a flight crew on standby. How much of a lead do they have on you?"

"A couple hours."

"Then it'll be tight," Carlyle said. "You'll want to hurry, and perhaps phone ahead to your colleagues at the airport."

"La Guardia or JFK?" she demanded. The two airports were almost equidistant from Brighton Beach.

"Kennedy."

"How do you know?"

"Erin, you haven't the time to go into how I know what I know," Carlyle said. "Will you trust me on this?"

"Yeah," she said. "Any idea where they'll land along the way? Small charters won't go all the way to Russia nonstop."

"Let me talk to a lad," Carlyle said. "Have you a number where I can reach you?"

She gave him her cell. "We're on our way to JFK," she said.

"Call me the second you have anything."

"Will do, darling. Drive safely." Carlyle hung up.

"What's up, Erin?" Jones called from the door of the command van.

"We've gotta go," Erin said. "JFK, right now."

"Hold it," Webb said, appearing behind Jones. "You're not going anywhere without my say-so."

"Vlasov's doing a rabbit," Erin said. "Private charter flight, according to my guy. We might still be able to stop him, but we have to get to the airport this second."

"ESU's not done with their sweep yet," Webb said.

"So leave them here! They don't need us."

Webb thought it over, then nodded. "Okay. I'm coming, too. Neshenko, you got room in your car for all of us?"

"It'll be tight," Vic said. "Four of us plus a dog. Get cozy." He moved as fast as his wounded leg would allow, sliding into the driver's seat. Webb took shotgun, as the second-biggest person in the car, and Erin and Jones squeezed into the back with Rolf between them. They didn't even have their doors shut when Vic peeled out of the parking space. He laid rubber and made for JFK along Belt Parkway, siren howling.

Webb was on the phone, first with Brooklyn and Queens police, then with airport security. Jones, meanwhile, was working her borrowed laptop, checking flight info.

"You sure they're flying out this way?" Jones asked. "Most charters need forty-eight hours' advance notice."

"These guys make their own rules," Erin said. "How many charter flights are going out tonight?"

"Hard to say," Jones said, typing away. "You know there's, like, two hundred international charters every year out of JFK."

"That's nice," Vic said over his shoulder. "Any other trivia you want to pass on?"

"They're not subject to the same baggage restrictions as

commercial flights," Jones said, missing the sarcasm.

"So they'll have guns in their carry-on," Erin said. "Fantastic."

"They still need passports and ID," Jones said. "Won't the airport catch them that way?"

"They'll have 'em under fake names," Erin said.

They were already close to the airport when Erin's phone buzzed in her pocket. She snatched it out.

"O'Reilly," she said.

"I've made inquiries," Carlyle said. "There's a charter to Iceland, Flight RKV36, that was booked by someone my lad describes as a very unsavory fellow with an accent from Eastern Europe."

"Kira," Erin hissed. "RKV36. Look it up!"

"He also says you'll be wanting to hurry," Carlyle said conversationally. "Since it's on the runway as we speak."

"Thanks," she said, hanging up. "Vic! Step on it! They're on the runway!"

"Keep your shirt on," he muttered, swinging onto the airport exit. "Hey, Boss, you want to tell the TSA what's going on?"

"Better try air-traffic control," Jones said. "Make sure they don't clear 'em for takeoff."

"Get us onto the runway," Erin suggested.

"Christ! One at a time!" Webb snapped. He tuned the car's police radio to the JFK air-traffic control frequency. "Better get out there, Neshenko. But be careful."

"It's illegal to drive on a runway without ATC approval," Jones pointed out.

"You shoulda been a lawyer," Vic said as he pulled up to the security entrance, braking so hard the tires squealed. "All that legal bullshit, wasted on a cop."

A couple of airport police trained flashlights into the car.

Vic showed them his shield.

"NYPD Major Crimes," he said. "We've got a warrant for a fugitive who's flying out right now."

The cop checked his shield number, just to be on the safe side, then opened the gate and waved them through. The airport was well-lit with enormous floodlights, but they had no idea which runway to make for.

Webb had finally gotten through to air-traffic control. Their response came over the car's radio for everyone to hear.

"Flight RKV36 has just cleared for takeoff on Runway 2," the controller said.

"Revoke their goddamn clearance!" Vic snapped.

"Stand by," the controller said with that maddeningly calm tone they always used.

"Straight ahead, a little left," Jones said. She had an airport map on her computer screen.

"NYPD vehicle," the controller said. "We are unable to raise RKV36 on radio. They are proceeding with takeoff."

"We're going onto the runway," Webb said. "We're a black Taurus. You see us?"

"Affirmative, NYPD," the controller said. "We are halting all taxi traffic on the runways in front of you. Continue on bearing three-five-zero."

"There they are!" Webb snapped, pointing. A small jet was almost straight ahead. It was pointed down the runway, about to start its takeoff run.

"Got it," Vic said, accelerating. "Let's play chicken."

*   *   *

Vic swung the Taurus across an access road onto the runway just behind the jet. His flashers painted the fuselage red and blue as he pulled forward, flooring the pedal. The jet was revving to take off. As the car passed the plane, Erin heard the roar of the aircraft's engines over the siren.

The charter jet was too low to the ground for them to slip under the wing. Vic swerved around the wingtip and back in front of the plane. Then he went into a fast skid. The car slid sideways, coming to a stop square in the middle of the runway. The plane was bearing down on them, the nose angled at them like an incoming missile.

"You did not just do that," Jones whispered.

"Out!" Erin shouted. They piled out of the car from every available door, Rolf scrambling after Erin. Vic grabbed his rifle from its place between the front seats. His leg buckled under him and he went to one knee. He rolled to the side and came up, aiming the gun at the plane. Erin reached for her Glock.

It wasn't there, of course. It was in an evidence locker.

"Shit." She didn't have a gun. Neither did Jones. Webb had his .38 Special in his hands, but one handgun and one rifle was hardly going to be enough.

At least they'd stopped the plane. It slowed, then came to a standstill, engines still idling. They were too low under the nose to see into the pilot's compartment, but Erin could guess how the pilot must be feeling.

"NYPD! Stop your engines!" Webb shouted, but there was no way anyone on the plane could hear him.

"Sir!" Erin screamed, practically in his ear. "I don't have a weapon!"

Vic was moving along the nose of the plane toward the door. He shouted something she couldn't hear and waved her over to him.

She ran up behind him. "I'm unarmed!" she informed him.

"Right ankle," he said.

She crouched and pulled up his pant leg. Vic had a backup gun in an ankle holster, a Sig-Sauer P232 nine-millimeter. She drew the gun and chambered a round. The little pocket pistol felt like a toy in her hands, but it was a hell of a lot better than nothing.

The door of the plane swung open. Vic and Erin aimed at the opening.

A teenage girl stood there, hands raised.

"We got hostages!" Erin called to Webb, who was standing a few yards behind them and couldn't see into the aircraft's interior.

"Jump down!" Vic shouted at the girl, then repeated it in Russian. She either didn't hear him or was frozen in place. She was crying, her cheap eye makeup running down her cheeks.

A guy leaned around her, an arm around her neck. His other hand was holding a MAC-10.

"Gun!" Erin and Vic screamed in perfect unison. Erin drew a bead on what she could see of the man's head, but in the dim light, with the unfamiliar gun, she didn't trust a shot not to hit the girl.

The thug pulled the trigger. The submachine-gun fired so fast she didn't hear the individual shots. The range was extremely close, but the gunman was firing one-handed, without having the weapon properly braced. Bullets spattered the tarmac between Erin and Vic.

Vic ignored the incoming rounds. Carefully, sighting down the barrel of his M4 carbine, he squeezed the trigger once.

The man's head snapped back as if he'd been creamed with a baseball bat. The MAC-10 fired another short burst as his finger reflexively contracted. Then he toppled backward out of view. The girl stayed where she was. She put her hands over her mouth and shrieked.

Erin jumped for the bottom of the doorframe and pulled herself up. "Out of the way!" she snapped at the girl, but the hostage was in no condition to obey orders. At their feet was the body of the man Vic had shot.

The interior of the plane was dark, lit only by the running lights down the aisle. Erin took a quick glance between the seats and saw movement. Acting on reflex, she dove down and forward, taking cover behind the front row of seats.

An assault rifle opened up full-auto. The muzzle flashes were enormously bright, leaving purple after-images on Erin's eyes. Chunks of upholstery flew. Erin reached back without thinking, grabbed the elbow of the girl behind her, and yanked her to the floor. She didn't think the girl had been hit, but she wasn't sure.

"Erin! Get out of there!" Vic was yelling at her. With his injuries, he couldn't easily climb up after her.

Falling back wasn't a bad idea, but Erin wasn't immediately clear on how to manage a retreat. She kept her head down and shifted to the side, just in time. Another burst of automatic-rifle fire chewed through her cover right where she'd been.

She figured the gunman had a pretty good idea where she was, but the flash of his gun was probably wrecking his vision as much as hers, so he was firing basically blind. It was a shitty thing to bet her life on, but she didn't see much choice. He'd get her by dumb luck sooner or later if she stayed put. Gripping the Sig-Sauer in both hands, she leaned out into the aisle, sighting down the barrel.

She saw more muzzle flashes coming from between two seats about halfway back. Shifting her aim just a little above her opponent's gun, she pulled the trigger twice.

The rifle fire stopped. Erin, half-deafened, could still hear more women screaming. She didn't know if there were other enemies. There were definitely innocents all over the place.

"Friendly!" Webb called, coming up behind her. He'd managed to lever his paunchy body into the plane.

"Cover me," she said and started toward the back of the

plane, checking each row as she went.

She found six young women, all of them riding a heavy dose of drugs and panic. In the row she'd taken fire from, a man was slumped on a seat. He was one of the big, blond guys who'd been guarding Vlasov at the restaurant. She recognized the calmer one, the one Tatiana had said was Russian special forces. He still had his rifle, an AK-74, in one hand. A bullet hole had been punched through his forehead just over his left eyebrow. His eyes were wide open, staring right at her.

Erin stared back for a second. She knew she should feel something, and figured she probably would as soon as everything was over, but right then, she was just glad he wasn't still shooting at her. She pulled the gun out of his limp fingers, laid it on the floor, and moved on to the next row.

It was the emergency exit row, over the wing. The door was standing open. Erin, cursing, ran to the doorway.

Peter Vlasov was on the wing, working his way toward the tip.

"NYPD!" she shouted, taking aim. "Put your hands in the air!"

Vlasov looked over his shoulder and made eye contact with her. In his face she saw so much fear that she almost felt sorry for him for a second. Vic had been right after all. He was a bully and, without his goons, a coward.

"Hands up!" she shouted again.

Vlasov started turning toward her. His left hand was in the air, but his right hand was low, inside his coat.

Erin fired.

Vlasov folded over and collapsed on the wing, clutching at his belly. He lay there, writhing in pain. Erin kept the gun pointed at him. To her own surprise, her hands were perfectly steady.

"Clear behind!" Webb said.

"Clear," she replied.

Webb came up beside her, pointing his revolver at the downed man. "Was he armed?" he asked.

"I... I think so," Erin said. The thought hit her, what if he'd just been reaching for a cell phone or something? She remembered every news story about every man who'd been holding his wallet when a cop had shot him. "He had his hand in his coat. I thought..."

"Let's check him," Webb said. The two detectives stepped out onto the wing, walking carefully. The aluminum was springy under their feet, the wingtip bouncing slightly with every step.

Vlasov was in too much pain and shock to understand a word they were saying. Webb crouched in front of the wounded Russian and patted down the man's coat. He felt something, reached in, and drew out an automatic pistol. Wordlessly, he held it up for Erin to see.

All the tension went out of Erin when she saw the gun. She leaned against the fuselage and wiped sweat from her forehead. She felt lightheaded and a little dizzy, but her hands still didn't shake.

Airport police vehicles were closing in. There really was nothing quite like the cavalry arriving late, Erin thought sourly. Just in time to help pick up the bodies. Webb was on his phone, calling for an ambulance. Vic limped into view on the runway below the wing. He stared up at Erin. They shared a long look. Then he nodded to her.

She nodded back.

Chapter 17

"Four suspects dead, two more wounded, one injured detective, and a destroyed police vehicle." Lieutenant Andrew Keane, NYPD Internal Affairs, leaned across his desk, fingertips forming a steeple in front of him. "What are your thoughts?"

"They're in my report, sir," Erin said.

Two days, mostly full of paperwork, had passed since the shootout at the airport. She and Keane were in his office on the fourth floor of Precinct 8. The youngest Lieutenant in the NYPD smiled thinly at her. Everything about him was sharp. His nose, the tilt of his eyebrows, and his eyes, so dark brown they were almost black.

"You haven't shot anyone before, have you?" he asked.

Erin felt a twinge of irritation at his mind games. He knew the answer as well as she did. He knew everything in her file. "I've shot two other men, sir," she said. "One during the art gallery heist, the other at Frankie Fergus's bar."

Keane was still smiling. "You know what I mean, Detective. This is the first time you've killed anyone."

"Yeah," Erin said.

"Are you handling it okay? You sleeping all right?"

"I've had my psych eval," she said. *Which you also know, asshole,* she thought but didn't say.

"Of course," Keane said, glancing at her personnel file where it lay on his desktop. "I just have a few questions for you."

Erin waited for him to ask them.

"Why didn't you let the airport police handle things at JFK?"

"It was our job," Erin said. "I wanted to see it through."

"You'd been in a gunfight just a few hours before," he said. "You nearly got killed. Your car was annihilated. Hadn't you done enough for one night?"

"I've never asked other officers to pick up my slack," Erin said.

Keane's smile turned into a grin. "I agree," he said. "In fact, looking at your file, one could get the impression that the opposite is true. Now, looking at your actions in the Brighton Beach shooting, I don't think there's anything you need to worry about. You were taking fire before you even got out of your car. CSU is still working the angles on the scene, trying to figure out whose bullets killed Paul Ivanov, yours or Detective Neshenko's, but it hardly matters. In any case, you used entirely appropriate force given the situation. I believe you will be receiving a commendation for valor.

"Now, with respect to the airport, how did you know where to go?"

"A tip from one of my CIs."

"Which one?"

"Sir," Erin said carefully, "if I toss his name around, he won't be very confidential."

"You don't trust my discretion?" Keane asked, raising one of his eyebrows.

"He wouldn't," Erin said. "He deals with a lot of underworld types. If word gets out that he gave a tip to a cop, his life might be in danger."

"I see," Keane said. "And I admire your personal loyalty. It's a scarce commodity these days, and refreshing to encounter. I'll be talking with Detective Neshenko, of course, about any reckless endangerment he may have perpetrated by, ah, parking a car in front of a moving jet aircraft."

"They were about to take off," Erin said. "We had to stop them. Vic—Detective Neshenko—just did what he thought he had to do."

"Personal loyalty," Keane said again. "Don't worry, Detective. This isn't a headhunting expedition. We just have to perform our due diligence. After all, someone may look through these files someday. We don't want them to think there was some sort of departmental coverup, do we?"

"Just ask the rest of your questions," Erin said, adding "sir," as an afterthought.

"Have it your way, Detective. Why did you climb onto an airplane you knew contained armed men who were perfectly willing to shoot at police?"

That was an easy one. "The girl," she said. "If they had one girl on board, there were probably others. Vlasov had killed witnesses in the past. I thought their best chance for survival was if we went in right away."

"What were you thinking at that moment?"

"Honestly, sir?" Erin said. "I was wishing I had a backup piece of my own, so I didn't need to borrow Vic's. I wasn't used to the Sig-Sauer. I was hoping I didn't miss."

He actually laughed at that. "I suppose you'll be carrying a backup gun from now on."

"Absolutely." Erin wasn't laughing.

"Did you want to kill Vlasov?"

The question came out of nowhere. "What?"

"It's a simple question," Keane said, but his eyes had

narrowed and hardened. "You knew he was a pimp, a kidnapper, a rapist, and a murderer. When you had him in your sights on the wing of that airplane, did you want to kill him?"

Erin thought it over. Those dark eyes drilled into her. She wondered what the right answer was. Then she thought, the hell with it, and told him the truth.

"I wanted to take him in," she said. "I wanted to slap the cuffs on him and see the look on his face when the cell door slammed shut behind him. I wanted to swing it extra-hard, make it really echo, so he knew for damn sure he was never getting out. I didn't want to shoot him dead. That would've been too easy. For both of us."

"Have you spoken to the hospital about him?" Keane asked.

"Yeah. They say he'll live."

"Yes, I've read the medical report," Keane said. "They had to resection his bowel and pump him full of antibiotics to stop sepsis from setting in. He may be carrying a colostomy bag around Sing-Sing with him." The Lieutenant's eyes lost some of their hardness, taking on a hint of amusement. "Lots of people talk about tearing someone a new asshole, Detective. You're the first one I know of who's actually done it."

"I was aiming center mass," Erin said. "I overcompensated for the recoil and hit low. Unfamiliar gun, like I said." She was a little ashamed of the shot. Gut-shooting a man was a hell of a lousy thing to do, even to a bastard like Vlasov.

"Your commanding officer, Lieutenant Webb, clearly heard you order Vlasov to put his hands up twice before you fired," Keane said. "It's highly unusual for an officer to be involved in two shootings in the same night. You understand the need for scrutiny, I'm sure."

"Yes, sir."

Keane stood up. So did Erin. The Lieutenant extended his hand across his desk. Surprised, Erin took it and shook.

"Good work, Detective," he said. "I knew you had excellent potential. I'm glad to see you filling your appointed role with such..." He paused, searching for the word. "Zeal," he finished.

"Thank you, sir," she said.

"You're a credit to the force, O'Reilly," he said. "I'll continue to watch your career development with great interest. And enjoy the remainder of your administrative leave. As much as you can, that is. I suspect you're already itching to get back on active duty."

"Yes, sir," Erin said and got out of there.

*   *   *

Why was everyone so concerned with how she was feeling? Erin felt fine. Like Vic had said about himself, she'd done what she had to do. It hadn't been fun. It wasn't something she looked forward to doing again. But she'd keep strapping on her gun and her shield.

Her dad called the night after the incident. The NYPD hadn't released the names of any of the detectives involved, but Sean O'Reilly had a lot of friends in the department, and someone had passed him the word.

Erin was on her couch, one beer in her stomach, another in her hand, watching more reruns of "24." When her phone lit up with her parents' number, she almost didn't answer it. But that would just make her folks worry more.

"O'Reilly," she said.

"Hey, kiddo," Sean said. "How's it going?"

He'd always be a cop. He was leading with an open question, trying to get her to give up information without letting on what he already knew. "I think you know, Dad," she said.

"What do you mean?"

"Sergeant Malcolm," Erin said. "Desk officer at Precinct 8. You and he used to work together when he was in Queens."

"You really are a natural detective, kiddo. Yeah, Brendan called me. I know about the thing in Brooklyn. I know you're not hurt." He paused. "Not physically. I dunno. We hear all this stuff about this PTSD these days, you know... the emotional thing."

"Dad," Erin said. "Don't pretend to be a psych guy. You're no good at it."

"Hey," he said. "I just want you to know I'm here for you. I know how it gets out there."

"Shot many guys, have you?" The words popped out of her without any planning.

"You know I haven't," he said. "That's not the point."

"That's exactly the point," she said. She was suddenly angry, and she didn't even know why. "That's why you're calling me right now. You're worrying about your little girl 'cause she just shot three guys. Two of them are dead and the third's in intensive care. You know what, Dad? I carry a gun. I'm a cop. And every day I go out there, I know maybe I'm gonna have to use it. Didn't you realize that when I put on the shield?"

"Of course I know that!" Sean snapped. "I knew you might, I just hoped you'd never have to!"

There was a silence that stretched out long enough for both of them to think about what they'd just said. Then her dad said, much quieter, "I know other guys who've had to shoot suspects. It's never a good thing, never the way they wanted it to go. Killing's not supposed to be easy, Erin. We're not supposed to be okay with it. It's the worst thing people can do to each other."

Erin thought about Tatiana and some of the things the Russian girl had said. She wasn't sure that was true.

"The thing that bothers them the most," Sean went on, "is

wondering if they'd done something just a little bit different, could the day have ended without anyone on a slab at the morgue? It eats them up. And it's a stupid question."

"Is it?" she replied. "Dad, these guys could've given up. Or we could've held back at the airport. Backup was on the way. Once we stopped the plane, we could've waited for a negotiator, talked them down. I almost got myself killed, Dad, and I blew a guy's brains out."

"Stop it, Erin," her dad said, in the same tone of voice he'd used when she was acting out as a teenager. "The review board's gonna ask those questions, because that's their job. Your job was to bring in some dangerous guys and rescue some really unlucky young women. You did your job. The bad guys made their choice. You're right, they could've given up. But they didn't. That's not on you."

To Erin's surprise, she felt tears forming. She cursed herself for her lack of self-control, but her eyes kept leaking. "They were gonna kill Vic, Dad," she said. "And Tatiana, and all those other girls. I couldn't let them."

"Of course not," he said. "I'm sorry it happened. But I am so proud of you, kiddo."

"Thanks, Daddy," Erin said, a word she hadn't used in years.

"Anyway, I had to call," he said gruffly. He cleared his throat. "Your mother was worried about you. You know how she gets."

"Yeah, I do," Erin said.

"Well, don't be a stranger," he said. "Call anytime. And Mary says to be sure to check in on your brothers, especially Tommy. She worries even more about him."

"Sure thing, Dad."

"Goodnight, Erin."

"'Night, Dad."

* * *

Erin went downstairs from Internal Affairs to the Major Crimes office. A meeting with IA was one hell of a way to start the day, but she felt like it had gone reasonably well. Now all she had in front of her was another day of modified assignment, riding her desk.

She and a very bored Rolf had been wading through forms and reports for about half an hour when the elevator dinged and Vic limped onto the floor. He'd taken the previous two days off. The official story was that he was recuperating from his injuries, but Erin didn't believe it. Vic was a play-through-the-pain kind of guy. He was dealing with what had happened, and from the look on his face, he wasn't done dealing with it yet. He looked tired, beat up.

"Hey, Vic," she said. "Still standing?"

"Hey," he said without much enthusiasm, sinking into his chair.

They had the office to themselves. Webb was meeting with Captain Holliday, and Jones was down in Evidence dealing with the enormous pile of crap the CSU guys had brought in from the restaurant and apartments above.

"How's the arm and leg?" she asked.

"Fine."

Erin thought it over, then decided to bite the bullet. "The DA's office decided not to press charges on Tatiana," she said.

"I know. The ADA talked to me," he said, staring straight ahead at his black computer monitor.

Of course he had, Erin realized. Vic was the cop who'd been attacked. "I maybe shouldn't have busted her in the first place," she said.

He shrugged. "I should've seen the trap. Like you did."

"You couldn't have known she was working for them."

"You did," Vic repeated.

"Lucky guess," she said.

He did look at her then. "I don't think so. You know, I thought... she got me. Like maybe we had something."

"She tried to protect you," Erin said. "She was scared to death, and she still took a chance, warning you."

"Last minute," he said. "Shit."

They sat in silence for a couple of minutes.

"You know," Erin said, "one of the perks of being a cop they never tell you at the academy."

"What's that?" Vic said, not really listening.

"The way it really spices up your love life."

Vic didn't react at first. Then he actually managed a smile. "Paid vacations, too. All you gotta do is catch a couple bullets, they send you straight home."

"Or shoot a few off," she added. "Plus, we get to mix with high society."

"Every day's an adventure," he said.

Erin smiled back at him. "We're okay," she said.

"Yeah."

The elevator bell rang again. They looked up. The doors slid open to reveal Natalie Markov. She was wearing a classy black dress with a black hat angled on her head. She paused, took a deep breath, and walked toward them.

Erin stood up. Vic didn't.

"Ms. Markov," Erin said. "What can we do for you?"

"Detective O'Reilly," Natalie said. "I have come to thank you and the others for what you have done for us."

"Just our job, ma'am," Erin said.

"No," Natalie said with a decisive shake of her head. "You found the monsters who killed Gregory, and you punished them. For that I must thank you."

"Ma'am," Erin said. "There's something I should say.

Ludmila, the woman who was killed, was meeting Gregory for a reason."

"I do not need to know this," Natalie said.

"I think you do," Erin said. "The young woman was pregnant. She wanted her child to have a better life than she could give her. Gregory helped her escape from a terrible situation. She was grateful. She was going to give her child to the two of you to raise."

Natalie put a hand to her heart and murmured something in Russian, her eyes closed. Then she recovered her poise. "The men who killed them," she said. "Do you know why?"

Erin nodded. "They were afraid she'd tell someone about their operation, bring attention. I think they thought she was telling him about herself."

"Gregory was a hero," Natalie said.

"He risked his life to help two girls escape," Erin said. "Yeah, he was a hero."

That shut them both up for a minute.

"The newspapers, they say there are other girls?" Natalie asked.

"Yeah," Vic said. "We got seven off the plane. Plus Anna."

"That is good," Natalie said. "I would like to meet them, to do something for them."

"Their situation is a little awkward," Erin said. "They were brought into the country illegally."

"So what will you do? Send them back?" Natalie demanded, her eyes flashing.

"It's not up to us," Vic said. "It's an Immigration thing now."

"So you will do nothing? You save their lives, then you throw them away?"

"Hey," Vic said. He stood up.

Erin faced the Russian woman. "Ms. Markov," she said, "we can't save anybody. People have to save themselves, and each other. All we can give them is a chance." She was thinking fast. "These girls are minors. Their families need to be contacted, if it's possible. But if they okay it, or if the families can't be found, then the girls will need sponsorship."

Natalie nodded. "But for this they must be relatives, yes?"

"It's not a requirement," Erin said. "They need someone to file an affidavit, promise to take financial responsibility until they become citizens."

Natalie crossed her arms, thinking it over. "Very well," she said. "I will do it."

"They won't let you sponsor all of them," Vic said.

"Then I will take as many as I can," she retorted. "And I will find others, good people, to sponsor the rest of them. Gregory gave his life to help people to come here and live. To honor him, I will do what he would do."

Vic glanced at Erin. "It'll be messy," he said. "And complicated."

"But it might work," Erin said. "Ms. Markov, I'll find out who you need to talk to, who can get you the right paperwork."

Natalie smiled a grim, determined smile. "Always there is the paperwork," she said. "I will do this, for Gregory, and for these poor girls. They will have a life, the best life I can give to them." She looked the detectives over. "You are a good man and a good woman. Thank you for this, and for everything."

"Thank you, ma'am," Erin replied. She offered her hand.

Natalie ignored it. She took hold of Erin's shoulders and kissed her on the cheek. Then she did the same to Vic, turned, and walked back to the elevator.

"That's some woman," Vic said as the doors slid shut behind her.

"They make 'em tough in Russia," Erin said.

"She's gonna be fine," he said. "And so will they."

"Eventually," Erin said.

"Eventually," he agreed.

Chapter 18

Erin had one more task to take care of before she closed her personal file on the case. At the end of the day, she went home, took Rolf for a walk through the neighborhood, and made her way to the Barley Corner. Not a single seat was available when she got there. But she saw Carlyle in his usual spot. By the time she got to him, he'd noticed her and made meaningful eye contact with the guy on his left. That man moved off without a word.

Carlyle stood. "Good evening, Erin. Have a seat, if you please."

She settled onto the stool, Carlyle resuming his own seat. Rolf settled under the bar at Erin's feet. Danny appeared, with his usual bartending magic.

"What'll it be, Erin?" he asked.

"Gimme a White Russian."

"And a Glen D whiskey for me," Carlyle said. "On the rocks."

While Danny made the drinks, Carlyle studied Erin's face. His eyes were thoughtful. He was taking in everything in her manner and appearance.

"What?" she said at last. She was starting to feel awkward.

"It's a funny thing," he said. "In your world, after what happened, you've all manner of reports to file, investigations into your conduct. Were you on the other side of the line, you'd have made your bones."

"Is that what this is to you guys? Some sort of test?"

"Maybe," he said. "But personally, I don't see that being a killer makes a lad either more or less trustworthy than he was the day before. I think it's more a matter of knowing yourself."

Erin's drink was waiting for her on the bar. She took a slug. "What do you mean?"

"The great mass of humanity wonder what they'd do in a life-or-death situation," he said. "Some, a few, discover the answer. Now you know something about yourself that you didn't."

She looked into his eyes. They were a clear, intense blue. "So what do you think?" she challenged him.

He smiled. "Erin, I already knew what you had in you." He took a drink of his whiskey, then swirled the ice cubes in the glass. His smile faded. "I told you the Russians were rough lads. I'm sorry things went the way they did."

"Are you?"

"Aye," he said. "Believe it or not, I was trying to help you."

"You did help," she said. "And that's why I'm here. I came to thank you."

"My pleasure."

It was her turn to study him. "You're different than any gangster I've ever met," she said.

His eyebrows went up. "Is that a compliment?"

"You've got a code," she said. "It's different from mine. Hell, it's different from everyone else's. But you've got it, and you stick to it."

"Maybe I do, at that," he said. "Does that surprise you?"

"I thought you were more selfish than that."

"Are you saying I'm a good man, in spite of my bad impulses?" He smiled more widely than before.

She grinned back. "No, you're still one of the bad guys. But you're not all bad."

"I suppose that's something," he said.

"We were able to save eight young women," Erin said.

"They'll have a rough time of it," Carlyle said. "But they're accustomed to difficult times, I imagine."

"Why do you care what happens to them?" she asked.

"I don't suppose you'd believe me if I said it was pure altruism?"

"Not for a second."

"What if I said I didn't know why I helped you?"

"I don't believe that either," Erin said. "Carlyle, I don't think there's a single thing you do or say without knowing exactly why."

"Fair enough," he said. He drained the rest of his whiskey and brought the glass down with a clink of ice cubes. "You've read my file, of course. When you were investigating me regarding the death of that unfortunate gambler."

She nodded.

"Then you know about Rose McCann."

"Your wife."

"It was those paramilitary bastards in the UVF," Carlyle said. "They came to our flat while I was out, looking for me, I expect. But they may simply have been targeting Catholic civilians. They did a great deal of that, you know. They shot my poor lass almost to pieces. I found out from the doctor, afterward. Erin, she was pregnant."

Erin swallowed. "I'm sorry," she said. It sounded as inadequate as it always did. Cops did too much breaking of bad news.

"We never did find the ones responsible," he said.

"So that's why you helped me."

He shook himself free of his memories. "No, Erin. I helped you because you asked me. I like the thought that you might come through the door of my pub every now and again. You raise the tone of the place."

"You are so full of shit, Cars," she said. "You make it sound good, 'cause you're a smooth SOB, but it's still bullshit. You should've been selling cars, instead of blowing them up."

He chuckled. "I'll not try to convince you otherwise, darling. There's no greater waste of time on this earth than trying to convince someone to believe something different from what they've already decided."

She finished her White Russian and stood up. Rolf jumped up, ready to go. She reached into her pocket.

Carlyle raised a hand. "Please, darling. I've told you before. Don't insult me by trying to lay money on my bar."

"Thanks for the drink."

He rose, ever the old-world gentleman. "Always a pleasure. I'm sure I'll be seeing you here again."

"Of course," she said. "Give an Irish girl a place she can get a free drink, she's sure to come back."

"If that's all it takes, it's more than worth it," he said. "Enjoy the rest of your evening, Erin."

For a long, strange moment, Erin was sure he was going to bow, or kiss her hand, or something. Then she got Rolf's leash and made for the exit. She didn't look back, but she knew he was watching her go.

* * *

The sidewalk under Erin's feet was warm, giving back the heat of the day. For a few minutes, she wondered what it would be like to be a civilian, just an ordinary woman walking her dog.

To be done at the end of the work day. To go home to dinner, maybe a husband and a couple of kids. Not to watch every passerby, scanning for a threat. Glancing in their faces, but mostly watching their hands. What will hurt you? Hands will hurt you. That was the first thing they taught you at the Academy.

Little flashes of memory sparked in her brain. The first bullet hole punching through the windshield of her Charger. The tear-streaked face of the girl on the plane. The wide-open eyes of the man she'd shot, and the tiny hole in his forehead.

Even if she wanted to do something else, it was too late. She was a part of the dark side of the world, and it was part of her. And the crazy thing was, in spite of all the horrible things she'd seen, and even done, she didn't want to do anything else. Erin O'Reilly was a cop. It was what she was born to do, just like Rolf was born to be a police dog. And God help her, she loved it.

"You and me, buddy," she said to the Shepherd. He cocked his head, but when orders weren't forthcoming, he went back to sniffing a signpost.

They got to the steps leading to Erin's apartment. As she turned toward the door, she saw a man walking toward her from the opposite direction. There was an instant of alarm. He was looking right at her and moving purposefully. But then she recognized his bright red hair and wide, mischievous smile.

"Erin, love!" he said. "What a grand surprise!"

"Corky," she said. "I suppose you're going to tell me this is a coincidence?"

James Corcoran spread his hands in a gesture of innocent surprise that didn't fool her one bit. "Perish the thought. I'd heard you'd moved into the neighborhood and hoped our paths might cross. As a matter of fact, I was just on my way down to the local public house. I thought I might drop in and see if you were going the same way, perhaps share a drink with a lonely lad?"

She laughed. "Corky, lonely is the last word I'd use to describe you." Then her detective's brain snatched at something he'd just said. "Hold on. How'd you know where I live? You've been to my old place in Queens, but not here."

"People talk," he said. "Ask a question here, find an answer there."

"Yeah, I don't buy it. Have you been following me?"

"Like a lovesick pup," he said cheerfully. "But only in my heart. No, truth to tell, I spoke with your landlord."

"Jesus," Erin said. "So much for having an unlisted address."

"Not to worry," Corky said. "He's an old mate. I've known Harris for years. He's reliable. But what about that drink?"

"Sorry to disappoint you," she said. "Rolf and I just came from the Corner. I've had my drink for the night."

"Erin, the night's not even begun. How can you be done drinking already? I'm starting to think you may not really be an Irishwoman."

She shook her head. "Not tonight, Corky."

"Tomorrow, then?"

"I don't think so."

He was still smiling. "You're turning me down?"

"Yeah."

"Afraid you'd do something you'd regret in the morning?"

Looking him over, Erin thought that might just be true. "You're with the O'Malleys," she said instead. "You're a gangster. I'm a cop. Even if I never catch you for anything, it'd never work out."

"How do you know that, if you've never tried it?"

"I've never taken a bullet to the gut. But I still know it'd hurt."

He gave her a pained look. "You really think it would be that bad?"

She shook her head again, but smiled as she did. "Good-night, Corky."

"Half a moment," he said. "One question."

She paused, half-turning away.

"Is it that big Russian lad? Afraid he'll be jealous?"

"What?" She was genuinely baffled. "Vic? You think I'm sleeping with *Vic?*"

It was Corky's turn to be confused. "You're not?"

"No!" Erin exclaimed. "He's my partner, Corky! It'd be like... God, like sleeping with one of my brothers!"

"Ah," Corky said. "Well, that's my mistake, then. Just promise me something."

"What?"

"You're too fine a lass to go all to waste," he said, winking. "Get yourself a fine lad. And if you don't, then do give me a call. I'm not hard to find."

Those words jogged Erin's mind again. "Corky," she said. "Did you lean on Harris to get me this apartment?"

"Word of honor, Erin, I'd nothing to do with it."

Erin nodded thoughtfully. She didn't think Corky told very many outright lies, but that didn't mean what he said was the whole truth. "I'll see you around," she said.

"I've no doubt."

"Stay out of trouble, Corky."

"Back at you, Erin."

She climbed the stairs to the lobby of her building, Rolf beside her. Somehow, she didn't think she'd be able to follow her own advice. Trouble had a way of finding her.

Erin squared her shoulders. She'd be ready for it, whatever came her way.

"Don't worry, boy," she said to Rolf. "We can take it."

Rolf wagged his tail.

Here's a sneak peek from Book 4: Double Scotch

Coming Winter 2018

"Rolf! *Fass!*" Erin O'Reilly snapped.

Her partner sprang into action. His feet barely touched the ground as he charged. The perp didn't try to run. That was smart; Rolf was faster than any man in New York. Instead, the poor guy threw his arm out in front of himself.

Rolf had him. His teeth snapped shut on the man's arm. With a terrific snarl, all ninety pounds of German Shepherd piled into the guy. As Rolf drove his target in a stumbling backward sprawl, the dog's tail wagged enthusiastically. He was having a great time.

"Okay! Okay!" the victim said. "I give up!"

"Rolf! *Pust!*" Erin ordered, giving the command in the dog's native German. Rolf obediently let go of the man's sleeve and returned to Erin's side, tail still wagging. "Good boy," she said, holding out his favorite tug-rope. Rolf immediately clamped his teeth on the toy and began happily dragging at it.

"Good boy?" Vic Neshenko echoed, brushing at the sleeve of his bite-suit. "He almost bit clean through."

"Sure," Erin said, still engaged in her tug-of-war with her K-9. "You're supposed to feel it. If he doesn't bite hard, then what's the point?"

"I got an idea," her fellow detective said. "Next time, you wear the suit, I'll give the orders. We'll see how you like that."

"I've been in the suit," she said. "K-9 school, everybody wears the suit sometimes, to help the other guys train their dogs."

"Like Tasers," Vic muttered. "Gotta ride the lightning before they let you carry 'em."

"At least they don't have the same rule for sidearms," Erin said.

That shut both of them up for a minute. It had been almost a month since their gunfight at JFK Airport. Erin and Vic had both killed men that night. They'd been clean shootings—as clean as taking a life could be—but it was something neither of them really wanted to talk about.

Now they were in Central Park, taking advantage of an unseasonably cool late-July day to get some outdoor training done. Erin worked Rolf every day, but she was the one person on earth he would never bite, so she needed to partner up for bite-work. Vic hadn't exactly jumped at the opportunity, but Vic wasn't jumping at anything these days. His bullet wounds had healed nicely, so that he hardly limped at all, but his spirit had taken a beating.

Erin worried about him. Vic had always been a surly guy, but since the Russian case, he'd been downright unpleasant. She knew why. It was his girlfriend. Ex-girlfriend, of course. The Russian girl had set him up to be killed. Even though it hadn't been her idea, or her choice, and she'd tried to walk it back, the experience had left Detective Neshenko with an even worse view of human nature than he'd had before.

Erin wanted to help him, but wasn't sure how. Hell, she had her own issues. The first week after the shootings, she'd had nightmares every single night. She kept waking up in a cold sweat, seeing muzzle flashes in the dark, grabbing for her Glock automatic in the nightstand. She hadn't shot any holes in her ceiling. Thank God for good trigger discipline. The dreams had spaced themselves out lately, and her temper wasn't flaring up like it had, but she knew she wasn't quite herself yet.

"At least it's been quiet," she said to fill the silence. Their Major Crimes unit hadn't had anything on their plate for nearly a week. That was one reason Lieutenant Webb hadn't objected to them taking some time out of the office.

"Great," Vic said. "Just fantastic."

"What?" she said. "You get tired of moping around, ready to get off the bench?"

"I don't mope," Vic said.

"What do you call it, then?"

"I'm Russian," he said. "We brood."

He smiled. Just a little, but it was a smile, and that was progress. Maybe there was hope for him.

"So you hoping we catch a case?" she asked.

"Beats being a chew-toy," he said. "I'm sick of sitting around doing nothing."

Rolf, realizing Erin's heart wasn't in their game, stopped tugging on his rope. He held it in his mouth and stared over it at

Erin. His tail went back and forth in a slow, hopeful wave.

Erin's phone buzzed in her pocket. *"Pust!"* she ordered Rolf, who let go of the rope at once. She fished out the phone and saw Webb's name on the screen.

"O'Reilly," she said.

"You got Neshenko with you?" her commanding officer asked.

"Most of him."

"Okay, the two of you get down to Corlears Hook Park," Webb said.

"What've we got?" she asked.

"Looks like a double homicide," he said.

"On our way," Erin said, disconnecting. She looked at Vic. "Looks like you got your wish. Time to go back to work."

*   *   *

Corlears Hook lay on the southeastern edge of Manhattan, on the bank of the East River. By the time Vic, Erin, and Rolf arrived, in Erin's brand-new unmarked police Charger, the uniforms had established a perimeter of yellow tape. Half a dozen officers were there, along with a couple of unnecessary paramedics who were finishing packing up their gear.

Detective Kira Jones waved them over to the shoreline. She'd recently re-dyed her hair, a habit picked up from her days as a liaison with the gang task force. Its tips were a bright, electric blue that made it easy to pick her out of a crowd.

"Where's the LT?" Erin asked.

With Levine," Jones said, gesturing with her thumb. "We just got here."

Sarah Levine was the Medical Examiner. She and Lieutenant Webb were standing near the water's edge, staring at a couple of lumpy shapes wedged in among the rocks. Levine was wearing a white lab coat, wire-rimmed glasses, and a thoughtful expression. Webb had his hands on his hips and a cigarette clamped in the corner of his mouth.

"What've we got, Sir?" Erin asked, stepping carefully on the slippery stones. Rolf, catching the scent, alerted her to the presence of a dead body.

"Two victims," Webb said. He took the cigarette from his mouth and used it as a pointer. "Jogger saw the crows going at them, wondered what was there."

"Where's the runner?" Vic asked.

"Going over her statement," Webb said, cocking his head. "She didn't see much. As soon as she figured out she was looking at bodies, she called it in."

Erin peered past Levine at the bodies. She couldn't make out much. "What do you think, Doc?" she asked.

Levine didn't look at her. "They were washed up here," the ME said. "This isn't where they died."

"Two bodies, washed up together?" Erin said. "That happen often?"

"Depends on the currents," Levine said. "I'll need to look at the charts."

"What are the chances they're related?" Erin said.

"Won't know till I do the bloodwork," Levine said. "They're both adult males, so it's possible they might be brothers."

"What I meant," Erin said, "is, are we looking at separate incidents?"

"Unlikely," Levine said. "Judging from the condition of the bodies, they probably went into the water at about the same time. My best estimate, until I study them further, is that they died within the last twenty-four hours, probably between ten and midnight."

"Accident, or foul play?" Erin asked.

"Check the hands," Vic said, entering the conversation.

Erin followed his look. The body he was examining was face-down. Its hands were secured with a cheap plastic zip-tie.

"Tied up," Webb said. "Definitely homicide."

Erin bent over to see more closely. "There's something wrong with that hand," she said.

"All five fingernails have been torn off," Levine said.

"Could that have been caused by something in the water?" Erin asked. She thought she knew the answer already, but she was hoping to hear different.

The other three all shook their heads. "Torture," Vic muttered.

"Preliminary cause of death is a single gunshot wound to the back of the cranium," Levine said. "I'd guess it was a handgun, thirty-eight caliber, or maybe nine-millimeter."

"The other one?" Webb asked.

"The other body presents identically," Levine said. "The hands are secured behind the back, a single gunshot wound to the head. The only difference is that both hands on the second one are intact."

"Tied up, interrogated, and executed," Webb said. He rubbed the bridge of his nose. "Then chucked into the river. We know where they came from?"

"Again, I'll need to check a chart of the currents," Levine said with a touch of annoyance.

"Could've come from anywhere," Vic said. "Bridge, boat, whatever."

"You got all the pictures you need?" Webb asked Levine. One of the ME's lab-techs was snapping shots of the corpses from every possible angle.

"Not quite," Levine said. "We need a few more minutes."

"Okay, get them out of the water as soon as you're done," he said. "We need IDs on them ASAP. And I want you back in the lab right away."

Levine gave him a curious look. "Where else would I go?"

He sighed. "Never mind. I want you to double-check cause of death. Get me a bullet, if the rounds didn't exit the skulls. Print 'em, check dental records. And get started on the clothes, see if we've got fibers, chemicals, anything that didn't wash out in the river."

Levine's annoyance was becoming more obvious. "Lieutenant, I do several examinations every week," she said. "I have a medical doctorate."

"Okay, okay," Webb said, holding up his hands. "I just want you to move this one to the head of the line. Anything you can tell us will help."

"How cold was it last night?" Erin broke in. She was still looking at the bodies.

"Seventy-five, give or take," Jones said. "Why?"

"These guys are dressed pretty warm," Erin said. Both dead men were clad in wool sweaters, one gray, one dark green. The body on the left also had a watch cap on his head. The bullet hole had entered his skull just below its edge.

"Yeah," Webb said. "Sailors, you think?"

"Looks like it," Vic said.

"That raises a question of jurisdiction," Jones said.

"Our bodies, our problem," Vic said.

"We're Major Crimes," Webb reminded her. "It doesn't matter where the body came from."

"It matters if they were on a ship over the Jersey border," Jones said. "The state line runs through the harbor, and depending on where the boat was at the time they were killed, if we can even figure that out. Of course, it's probably a Port Authority matter in any case..."

"Oh, for Christ's sake," Vic said.

"Until we know where they came from, they're ours," Webb said. "You really want to worry about that bureaucratic bullshit now?"

"I thought that was your job, Sir," Erin said with false innocence.

"May you make Lieutenant someday," Webb said. "And may you on that day be blessed with detectives of your own, just like you."

"I bet he says the same thing to his kids," Jones said out of the side of her mouth.

"Not much of a crime scene," Vic said. "This is just where they fetched up."

"I agree," Webb said. "But we'll need the CSU guys to comb the rocks anyway, in case any other evidence washed up."

They all took a moment to look at the shoreline. Empty bottles, plastic bags, and all sorts of trash were scattered everywhere. Jones said what each of them was thinking.

"Those poor bastards."

Ready for more?

Join Steven Henry's author email list
for the latest on new releases, upcoming books and
series, behind-the-scenes details, events, and more.

Be the first to know about new releases in the Erin
O'Reilly Mysteries by signing up at
tinyurl.com/StevenHenryEmail

Acknowledgments

This book, as with all my others, is possible in large part because of the efforts and support of many other people.

First off, there's my publisher and editor, Ben Faroe, of Clickworks Press, and his wife Kristen. Ben has given me tremendous assistance in understanding the publishing world, both print and electronic, along with many hours of his time in editing, proofreading, and helping with cover layout and design. Thank you Ben for your instrumental support and guidance!

Thanks also to Bryan Beach for editing assistance and feedback. You caught some things that slipped through the net and provided valuable insights from your prior experiences. I'm so glad you enjoyed the book!

A big thank you and salute, as always, to the dedicated men and women of the Burnsville, Minnesota Police Department, not simply for helping me understand the life and experiences of a police officer, but for your hard work and sacrifice in keeping the streets of my home safe. Take care of yourselves out there. Thank you to all the members of the thin blue line who, like Erin O'Reilly, do their best to meet the difficult demands of policing, to protect, and to serve.

Thank you to my parents, Carl and Mary Caroline Henry, and my in-laws, Dave and Marilyn Lindstrom, for your first readings, your suggestions, and most of all, your unflinching and constant support.

A great big tip of the hat to the PI team: the diehards Ingrid Henry, Justin Moor, and David Greenfield; and those who were along for part of the journey: Hilary Murphy, Mark Murphy, Bridget Johnson, and Ben Lurie. You'll recognize some of the characters and events in this book. I hope I did them justice.

Thanks again Shelley Paulson for my author photo! You're a magician with a camera lens.

Last on the list, and first in my heart, thank you to my wife and number-one fan, Ingrid. You've put in countless hours on this project, listening to my rough drafts, laying out and designing the cover, and always being more than willing to talk over the world of Erin O'Reilly. Without you, none of this would ever have happened.

About the Author

Steven Henry learned how to read almost before he learned how to walk. Ever since he began reading stories, he wanted to put his own on the page. He lives a very quiet and ordinary life in Minnesota with his wife and dog.